W9-DJB-209

The intelligent choice for dining.

HARVARD BOOK STORE

THE MENU IS OUR BEST SELLER.

Breakfast through Late Dinner 8 a.m.-11 p.m.,
Closed Sunday

190 Newbury St. at Exeter, Boston   536-0095

SUBSCRIBE TO

CALLALOO

a tri-annual black south journal of arts and letters

CONTRIBUTORS

Alvin Aubert, Robert Chrisman, Jayne Cortez, Mari Evans, Julia Fields, Leon Forrest, Ernest Gaines, Michael Harper, Gayl Jones, June Jordan, Clarence Major, James Alan McPherson, Sterling Plumpp, Kalamu ya Salaam, Sonia Sanchez, Ntozake Shange, Quincy Troupe, Alice Walker, Margaret Walker, John Wideman and Al Young.

Photo: Robert Pass

Publishes poems, short stories, articles, short plays, interviews, photography, graphics, reviews, folklore, essays and reports on Black art and culture.

Send subscriptions and manuscripts (SASE) to:

Charles H. Rowell, Editor, CALLALOO
Department of English, University of Kentucky
Lexington, Kentucky 40506-0027

Please enter my subscription to CALLALOO:

Name _____

Address _____
street

_____
city   state   Zip

____ One (1) year/$10   ____ Two (2) years/$18   ____ Single issue/$5

(If outside the U.S.A., add $5.00 per year.)

The bookstore for those who appreciate the difference.

It's very easy to fill shelves with thousands of titles . . . but our reputation is based on more than that.

At Harvard Book Stores, our buyers take the time to find and keep in stock a high quality selection for a demanding literary audience. This is why we've been told we're a "different kind of book store."

For example . . . our Literary Criticism, Poetry, and Fiction Sections, just to mention a few, are outstanding. But, don't let us just tell you . . . come in and see for yourself.

We know you'll appreciate the difference.

Harvard Book Stores Inc.

1256 Massachusetts Avenue • Cambridge, Massachusetts 02138

Mastercharge & BankAmericard Accepted

Pym-Randall
Announces

MEGAN STAFFEL *A Length of Wire & Other Stories*
"This collection of honest and wise stories is a reminder of the continuing strength of the Pym-Randall Publishing programs and of the growing prowess of Megan Staffel. Her characters are tender, but not stupid or easy in a world that is not always generous." — *Frederick Busch, Colgate University.*
Paper, $6.00; Cloth, $12.00

FRANZ WRIGHT
The One Whose Eyes Open When You Close Your Eyes
"First books are supposed, at best, to show promise. Franz Wright shows promise and more: the beginnings of brilliance. Just as the poems in this book needed to be written, they need to be read." — *Thomas Lux, Iowa Writer's Workshop.*
Paper, $5.00; Cloth, $9.50; Signed Edition, $12.50

FROM OUR BACKLIST

FIVE NEW ENGLAND VOICES
RICHARD EBERHART *New Hampshire: Nine Poems**
MICHAEL S. HARPER *Rhode Island: Eight Poems*
THOMAS LUX *Massachusetts: Ten Poems*
IRA SADOFF *Maine: Nine Poems*
MARCIA SOUTHWICK *Connecticut: Eight Poems*
Wrappers, $3.00; Signed Edition, $10.00 (*Signed Sold Out)

GERARD MALANGA *Chic Death.*
With reproductions of "The Death Paintings" by Andy Warhol.
Paper, $3.00; Cloth, $6.50; Signed Edition, $12.00

GEORGE STARBUCK *Talkin' B.A. Blues; . . . How I Discovered B.U., Met God, and Became an International Figure.*
A Rhyming fiction. Paper,
$2.50; Cloth, $5.00; Signed Edition, $10.00

GEORGE STARBUCK *Elegy in a Country Church Yard.*
A concrete poem, fold-out. Boxed, signed edition, $10.00

STEPHEN TAPSCOTT *Penobscot: Nine Poems.*
Wrappers, $3.00; Signed Edition, $10.00

PYM-RANDALL PRESS
73 Cohasset Street
Roslindale, MA 02131

PLOUGHSHARES

Vol. 11, No. 1

DeWitt Henry
Peter O'Malley   *Directors*

Thomas Lux   *Coordinating Editor for this Issue*

Susannah Lee   *Managing Editor*

Ploughshares 11/2&3, a double fiction issue edited by James Alan McPherson and DeWitt Henry, is editorially complete. *Ploughshares 11/4*, an international issue for solicited work only, will be edited by Stratis Haviaras.

Ploughshares is published at Box 529, Cambridge, MA 02139-0529, with editorial offices at the Division of Creative Writing and Literature, Emerson College, 100 Beacon St., Boston, MA 02116 and at 214A Waverly Ave., Watertown, MA 02172 (phone 617-926-9875). The Publisher is Ploughshares, Inc., a non-profit, tax-exempt educational organization funded in part by

The National Endowment for the Arts, a federal agency

and by

The Massachusetts Council on the Arts and Humanities, a state agency.

Administrative services are supported in part by

Emerson College.

Additional support comes from private contributions, from volunteer help, and from donations in services and kind from the business community.

Subscriptions: 1985 rate $14 (domestic), $16 (foreign). Single copies $5.95. ISSN 0048-4474. Trade distribution by Bernhard DeBoer, Inc., 113 E. Centre St., Nutley, NJ 07110; Bookslinger, 213 East Fourth Street, St. Paul, MN 55101; and LS Distributors, 1161 Post St., San Francisco, CA 94109. Microfilms of back volumes available from University Microfilms, Inc., 300 Zeeb Rd., Ann Arbor, MI 48106. Back issues available from the publisher. Ad rates on request. Indexed in M.L.A. Bibliography, American Humanities Index, Index to Periodical Fiction, Index of American Periodical Verse, Book Review Index. Self-index through Volume 6 available from the publisher; annual supplements appear in the fourth number of each subsequent volume.

All manuscripts should be accompanied by a stamped, self-addressed envelope. We cannot be responsible for loss. Please mark "poetry," "fiction," or "essay" on outside of envelope and allow us some time to reply.

Typesetting by Xanadu Graphics, Cambridge.

©1985 by Ploughshares, Inc.

Contents

Cover Painting, "Tacit Witness" (oil on linen 84″ × 96″),
by David True

MFA

Writing Program at Vermont College

Intensive 12-Day Residencies
August and January on the Vermont campus.
Workshops, classes, readings ● Planning for 6-month
projects.

Non-Resident 6-Month Writing Projects
Individually designed during residency. Direct criticism
of manuscripts ● Sustained dialogue with faculty.

Degree work in poetry, fiction and non-fiction. Plus a post-
graduate writing semester for those who have already finished
a graduate degree with a concentration in creative writing. For
further information:

**Roger Weingarten ● MFA Writing Program
Box 508, Vermont College ● Montpelier, VT 05602**

Other opportunities for graduate and undergraduate writing
study are also available at the college. Vermont College admits
students regardless of race, creed, sex or ethnic origin.

Faculty:

Dianne Benedict	Gladys Swan
Susan Dodd	Leslie Ullman
Mark Doty	Gordon Weaver
Jack Myers	Roger Weingarten
Sena Jeter Naslund	David Wojahn

Visiting Writers:

Nicholas Christopher	Edward Hirsch
Carolyn Chute	Denis Johnson
Andre Dubus	Larry Levis
George Garrett	Naomi Shihab Nye
Jorie Graham	Gerald Stern
Patricia Hampl	Mary Swander
Richard Tillinghast	

THE COORDINATING COUNCIL
OF LITERARY MAGAZINES
ANNOUNCES THE WINNERS OF
THE 1984 GENERAL ELECTRIC FOUNDATION
AWARDS FOR YOUNGER WRITERS:

JOHN GODFREY
for poetry
published in
GANDHABBA
and **MAG CITY**,
New York.

PAUL HOOVER
for poetry
published in
**ANOTHER
CHICAGO MAGAZINE**,
Chicago.

MICHELLE HUNEVEN
for fiction
published in
WILLOW SPRINGS,
Cheney,
Washington.

TAMA JANOWITZ
for fiction
published in
MISSISSIPPI REVIEW,
Hattiesburg,
Mississippi.

MARGO JEFFERSON
for
a literary essay
published in
GRAND STREET,
New York.

RUDY WILSON
for fiction
published in
**THE PARIS
REVIEW**,
New York.

The awards recognize excellence in new writers while honoring
the significant contribution of America's literary magazines.
This year's judges were Doris Grumbach, Elizabeth Hardwick,
Kenneth Koch, James Alan McPherson and Gary Soto.
For information about
THE GENERAL ELECTRIC FOUNDATION AWARDS FOR YOUNGER WRITERS,
please write to: **CCLM, 2 Park Avenue, New York 10016.**

Line portraits by David Johnson.

Thomas Lux

Editor's Note

I last edited an issue of *Ploughshares* (Vol. 1/4) nearly 12 years ago. It was a pleasure doing it once more and I would be glad to do it again in the future—say, in another 12 years.

The emphasis in this issue is on younger/newer poets. In many cases, I chose to accept larger groups of poems than usually get printed in magazines. If I have any specific hope for this issue it is that other editors will discover some of the younger/newer poets represented here and be receptive to more of their poems.

James Tate

Tuesday's Child Is: Full Of Grace

Too soon she is the grandmother,
able to live only for others,
when what she wants is to be left alone.
This one, Tuesday's child, it's not that
she wants to die, nor does she live
on memories. For her, the past exists
no more than the future. She waits
and watches the body decay, the eye
cease to observe. Tuesday's child
is full of grace. The Lord exists
in her eye, with his only chance for fame.

Islands Of Lunch

Red snapper with tabouli,
I tucked the napkin into my drink.
Smooching broke out at the next table.

I am talking a luncheon language
to a Lebonese architect
posing as a recently divorced Finn
in the Peachtree Center.

Red snapper, until the species
cannot afford summer vacations,
lunching on the bottom,
farming among the lower brocoli.

"I am a pagan, I will always be a pagan,"
a faculty wife explains.

A determined waiter surfaces
with pastry fit for war.

"But Jim, I don't see how we
can afford to marry, I am just a poor
bookie who happens to be the sister
of Lawrence of Arabia, and you know

his insurance coverage wasn't that good."

Jo Jo's Fireworks — Next Exit

Past the turpentine camps,
brilliant green lamps held
by woozy militia men,
the car with a nose of its own,
with headlight-eyes, sniffs
through the mountain fog,
heart palpitating, belly
hungry for gasoline pancakes.
Ghettos rave in their sleep,
butchering alto solos,
harvesting white snakes.
The car, evermore threadbare,
feels lost on Chevrolet Avenue,
a victim of the Taxi Wars.
Salamanders glow like tiny cutlets
and each Inn is in secret
a detention barracks, each
exit an entrance to underground
cuniculi, concatenation
of clandestine suburbs
from which there is no escape
until dawn, when bellboys are young.

Dear Customer

"Before placing me on your shelf, please take me by the feet and give me a few hard shakes to help restore that 'just made' look. Thank you." I have been carrying these instructions around in my pocket for weeks, pulling them out at odd moments. I found them on the street and I don't know what they're for — perhaps a teddy bear's suicide note.

"Marrrrk," my wife yells at me, "Come here and tell me what the hell is coming out of the sink." It looks like some kind of puree of lizard.

This was to be our time, the rediscovery of one another as tender, loving beings, with a vague insinuation by our friends, who had been through the wars for twenty years, that we might even wake-up feeling nineteen years old, as when we first met, puppies in heat, blind heat.

"I'll just drive down to the hardware store and see if they have some of the bacteria that eats things like this. Miracle stuff, thrives on backed-up puke."

Shirley from next door is scratching at the kitchen window, her words ricochet off the double thermal panes and scare several flickers into the over-cast sky. Shirley is a perpetually depressed social worker who must smoke marijuana all day every day in order to put a dim sheen on her depression. But she seems to know something about this green stuff, or perhaps it is her own emergency whose import we fail to decipher.

"I'll just run down to Kentfield's and will be back with the stuff in a couple of minutes."

Florence looks at me, looks back at Shirley, who by now has collapsed out-of-view. The birds are back, completely oblivious to the nature of human suffering.

I've turned on the radio in the car. ". . . terrorism is the second largest industry. . . ." Well, of course, nowadays.

What with the wall-units and the lawn slaves, what can you expect. The parasites found in sushi. In my day, romance was quite an adventure. Tourism, I see, he meant tourism.

A man's place is in the hardware store. No place like feeling like a Dad as in the hardware store. I take my time. Examine the merchandise, all of which I want, none of which I know how to use. When I describe my problem, today's specific problem, the son of the son of the owner looks at me as if I were a vile fetishist about whom he had had precise warnings. "Forget it," I say, pretending absentmindedness. "What I really need today are some bass plugs. You've got fishing lures, haven't you?" And I am overcome with that sense of randomness that I had left the house to avoid, hoping beyond hope to find some firm ground here at Kentfield's, the old family hardware store. "Is your father working today?" I ask genially, as though the kid had made a real fool of himself.

"He died three years ago."

Before placing on the shelf, a few hard shakes. . . .

Florence and Shirley are having tea on the front porch. I've never seen two more serene faces. They don't need me. The lizard has retreated. No sign of a mess anywhere. Their world is temporarily ordered. Recipes, children, the operations of mutual friends, fabrics, fall chores, local politics. They don't even look my way when I slam the side door.

They don't care that I have gargled dirt since this day began.

Stella Maris

There was nothing to do on the island. The dogs chased glass lizards into the dense myrtle bush. I don't know how the children slept. Men and women did what they could to extinguish the brightness of the stars.

One night my own supply of rum ran out, and I paced the verandah of my little hut-on-stilts. A ship was passing, the air was warm and moist like an animal's tongue. The island had once been home to pirates and run-away slaves, and giant sea turtles that crawled out by moonlight to lay their eggs. I no longer remembered what brought me there. And always the sound of the sea, like an overtone of eerie applause, the clapping of the palms of the palmettos.

I was dreaming, slightly intoxicated, and I found myself standing outside the little Catholic church, Stella Maris, "Star of the Sea." The priest stood before me, a beaten, disshevelled man with ashes on his robes and the unmistakable aroma of alcohol like an unholy ghost drawing us closer.

"These people," he said, waving his arm around at his imaginary flock, "they think love's easy, something nice and tidy that can be bought, that makes them feel good about themselves. Believe me, it's a horrible thing to love. Love is a *terrible* thing, terrible!"

And I, an unbeliever, believed him. The next day the owner of the liquor store told me that the priest had been a Jew and a lawyer from New York before converting and becoming a priest assigned to this, the dregs of the Pope's Empire. Sharks and wild boar had thinned-out the unbelievers. And Father

Moser drank through the night, testing his faith with Fyodor Dostoevsky.

I never knew whether or not I had dreamed-up that black-hearted priest, but I left the island shortly, and only now look back at my darkest hour with nostalgia.

Made In Holland

Pigtails fiddles with my riverbed,
she shoots some plutonium up my harpsicord.
I am here in Holland up a nut tree.
I walk the shopping mall in my pajamas.
My cologne seems to intoxicate everyone.
Deluded cattle walk out of the barbershop
saying things like "Nice pajamas," and
"Didn't I see you at the golf club last week?"
"Alms," I say, "Alms for The Sacred Rifles.
Alms for The Pampered Daughters of the Dragonfly."
Papa's up a nut tree in Holland, Pigtails
reposes over the fretwork of his dominion.
I am tethered to some daft subterfuge.
A doorbell rings, but there is no door.
Chuckle. A buzz, a bundle arrives:
someone in clogs is bringing it toward me.
It is my fever they want. I reach for the mop
and fall, fall quaintly against fluffy sashes,
and I fall on Pigtails, prod her
bereaved haven, skim the blemish of her starch.
And that is why I am in Holland.
That must be why, tulip.

Richard Jackson

James Tate: Tipster Nomad on a Planet of Rough Edges

I

'The Strand of Dark Beginnings'

"But metaphor is never innocent. It orients research and fixes results," Jacques Derrida writes in *Writing and Difference* (17). And so for the poet who wishes to write a poetry of discovery rather than a mimicry or recitation of fixed forms of thinking, metaphor must subvert cultural and aesthetic expectations, unravel the expected results. For James Tate, especially in his latest two books (*Riven Doggeries*, *Constant Defender*), this has meant a poetry whose language is based increasingly on non sequitors, contradictions, literalized figures of speech, episodic detail from partially erased narratives, false causalities, associative leaps, askew parallelisms, and a whole tangle of other dismantling strategies. For him, the focus has always been on the mind's discovery of itself through such linguistic strategies. He says in a recent interview: "we enjoy colloquial speech because it brings things vividly alive instead of being homogenized by our culture. Setting that language in motion unsettles the reader in a deep way. The reader thinks that the poem is making a statement and then all of a sudden the poem insists that the reader think about words, not about content . . . It's up to the reader to gather the little shards of meaning from the friction set off by words being imposed on one another in a way that doesn't seem natural" (*Poetry Miscellany*, 12, p. 51). What the poems do, then, is dramatize a process of seeing and revaluing. Static meaning in the traditional sense of a simple paraphrase that centers the text is eschewed for a dynamics of mind and heart, the vagaries of our attachments to the world — in short, for a realism of the imagination. "Writing does not," Derrida says, "simply weave several threads into a single term in such a way that we might end up unravelling all the 'contents' just by pulling a few strings" (*Dissemination*, 350).

Tate's, then, is a poetry of mobility: "I would / have to disagree with me always, / miss a train in my head," he says in "I Got a Little Flat off 3rd & Yen" (*RD*, 34). In "The Human Eraser" (*RD*, 47) he writes: "My one minute stands up and salutes / a monument of strangled glass." The moment / monument, the life, gradually contains the whole of human history that also contains it. The meaning of things becomes "a terrible message that has stopped / searching for the perfect night." Such an overplus of language, a surplus of meaning, reveals, in the end, the role of undecidability and playfulness in Tate's work:

> This is a truth for pillows to sort:
> you know you don't know, falsehood
> curdles the poor limited planet
>
> like a dispirited angel thrashing
> her memoir, and spectacular lilies
> ill in an excess of earthly grace,
> too much care, ideal in dark taverns.

The 'subject' of Tate's poems is precisely the way our limited language behaves when confronted with a world that means always more than language can know.

For Tate, this does not suggest chaos, but rather that he must be engaged in a continual revisionary process, as in "The Horseshoe" (*CD*, 14), for example. This poem begins with the speaker examining an old scrapbook:

> I can't read the small print in the scrapbook:
> does this say, *Relinquishing all bats, feeling faint*
> *on the balcony?* There is so much to be corrected here,

> so many scribbles and grumbles, blind premonitions.
> How does one interpret, on this late branch, the
> unexpected?

Eventually he stumbles across "the heart-rending detail / of the horseshoe found propped against the windowsill." And it is precisely the details, or more correctly the "Years of toil to find the right angle," the right perspective to see the details, that becomes most crucial. And yet each detail also "sinks" away and the meanings, the pencilings, go *under erasure*, as Derrida says, or into a system of double writing:

> I see the corrections
> penciled in. I'm privy to their forgetfulness, a sprawling
> design: I look away and project streaks of hesitant chance
> wherever I look.

Finally, the poet's reading the past becomes, like his shaving which is so casually introduced, a way of scraping the past away to write it anew:

> I must take back your corrections to the mute
> and infirm stretches of my own big shave, swell the parallel
> world with your murky burden, still betting against this charm
>
> nailed to the sidedoor of a photograph to ward off, what was it,
> was it me?

In the end, the poet's strategy is revealed as a way of discovering a self, a history, a record of the self's struggles to read and rewrite a past. The moment, the poem, becomes one of continual interruptions, "a constellation / of my own bewilderment" (*CD*, 42), the record of unravellings, of life "in the heart of the periphery" (*CD*,   28).

II

'On To The Source'

How, then, does the poet begin in the midst of all these

unravellings, where everything is always already a rewriting?
"In the beginning," Charles Simic writes, "always a myth of
origins of the poetic act," always the desire to find that "place
of 'original action and desire,' to recover our mute existence,
to recreate what is unspoken and enduring in words" (*NLH*,
1977, p. 144). For Tate, this act of recovery involves a desire
to understand how the past is "constantly pressing on the
present" (*PM*, 51) and also to understand how the future, as
a sort of "destiny," leans at the same time back on that present. The focus, it is important to note, is always on the elusive present, the moment where there is "everything / at stake
for that instant" (*RD*, 4), and not on some simple nostalgia
for the past nor a wistful hope for the future. Tate's is a
poetry at once attached to and detached from larger struc-
tures of understanding, larger contexts of time, at once filling and emptying its moments, voiced and anonymous —

> And then for that one hour
> there are no familiar faces:
> this lovely misbegotten animal
> created from odd bits of refuse
> from minute to minute
> splits us down the middle.
>   *(RD, 6)*

It is this toughness of spirit that keeps the poetry from
sentiment, but it is also precisely by the verbal play, the
metaphoric hi-jinx, the jokes and undercuttings, that we can
measure how much of an intense longing is being screened
by the poems' surfaces — increasingly, it seems, in these
latest books. We could note, for example, how the shift in
syntax in the last three lines quoted above disrupts even as it
confirms the "splitting" in the last line. The poet becomes, as
Tate suggests in "the Shy One" (*RD*, 26), a "tipster nomad"
who is alone, who is subject to ominous "clouds" and
"chords" — "cruel chords remembering" —

> And because of this
> and so much more, I am allowed

> to scratch my way to the surface again:
> a fabulous homing instinct remains,
> and wounds.

But the end is always deferred: the poet becomes like the Doctor in "On To The Source" (*RD*, 40) who would "stop and forget to unravel his tale: / *On To The Source*, when he was there.

Just how unsettled and precarious the moment is, how bleak the "wounds" against which its language struggles, how intense the "homing instinct" is, becomes apparent in two poems from *Constant Defender*. "Tell Them   Was Here" (17) narrates the journey of the speaker back to an ancestral home where, he finds, "no one was home." And so he begins to brood —

> *Unreliable ancestors!*
> Then it was night and I began
> to doubt: It's all lies,
> I came from no one, nowhere,
> had no folks and no hometown,
>
> no old friends. I was born
> of rumors, a whisper in one
> state, a unsubstantiated brawl
> in another, uncontiguous state.

Rumors, whispers, the myths of the unsubstantial, these images that haunt *Constant Defender*, and to some extent the earlier work, are all the self has to go on. In response, the narrator, as poet, can only inscribe his name —

> Green was here, I scrawled
> on a scrap of paper, and stuck it
> inside the screen. Started to leave,
>
> turned, scratched out my name —
> then wrote it back again.

The signature — "Green" — possibility — scratched out, written over — a double writing; — the identity of the self is given in the very process of attempting to write, to discover (even by covering, scratching over, and uncovering) the self as something more than a reference to the fixed past of "unreliable ancestors." The self becomes whoever writes in this active, dynamic sense.

In a curious way, then, the self becomes its own ancestor, an ironic turn upon the Wordsworthian phrase; in "Nobody's Business" (16), the child actually does become visionary father of the man, though this complex point of view is withheld until the end. The poem begins:

> The telegram arrived
> and no one was there to read it.
> The hens shooed themselves from the porch,
> softly, with tentative pleas for rainwater.
> Inside, the house stiffened, halted in mid-flight.

As the poem continues, the language of spaces that are cold and empty modulates — "exits," "marginal concession," "numb monosyllables," "alcove," "props," "spacious recesses," "cold interior." In the end the scene is ironically, proleptically filled by a boy looking through a telescope to the future, the house, which is his own, one of isolation, abandonment, detachment from society:

> A child with his birthday telescope
> has observed all this. He tells no one,
> it is nobody's business. But nothing is forgotten.
> Clad only in fluid intervals, he is untouchable,
> mincing toward that housewarming
> that is surely his.

The irony here is almost unbearably grim, and would be overwhelmingly so if it were not for the language play earlier in lines like: "Spacious recesses tried imitating a troupe of mimes, / but it was not fair to the exits" (mimicing the mimicers, fair / far, spaciousness / exits (& confinement)). The lines become a comic parody of themselves, exiting the very meanings that hover around them, mincing and menacing at once.

An even greater spaciousness and the role of the self in it

becomes the drama of "Mystic Moment" (*CD*, 22). The narrator begins his meditation "from the window of a Pullman car" not with a linear analysis or description such as we would find, say, in Jarrell's "Moving," but with a haunting set of images that produce an overplus of associations suggesting a lush world and imagination — "a plush and velvet world / with plugs of tobacco / outside a jelly factory." Yet this world is also one of intense deprivation, a desert where "mountains had long ago crumbled away, / erased by some soft artillery on the radio." (It is worth noting that Tate's images usually have a very realistic base: in a way, radio waves do "flatten" mountains just as they "narrow" distances.) The complex of opposites in texture here helps support the sense that the self is confused between two worlds, one passing by the window, the other above in a "swarm of burnt out stars," the invisible ghosts of lost worlds. The sense of loss is climaxed in the poem when the narrator confronts a reflected other (also an important recurring image in the book):

> I thought I saw my twin, limbless on the desert,
> drowning near a herd of angels; I reached out the window
> and killed him in a single blow.

And yet, in spite of such violence, really against the self, the self persists, in the tracings of the language. Note, for example, the way the second line in the passage above, as a single unit, underscores the identification of the "I" and the "he" — the "I" both reaches and is outside, "drowning." In this way the self always also occupies another place, becoming, by its very amorphousness, what Tate calls "a nameless representative of humanity" (*PM*, 52).

The speaker becomes, as Tate says in "Blue Spill" (*CD*, 29), "the fatherless son and the sonless / father," in a place and time always elsewhere "where his new life / begins quietly in the eyes of a wakened animal." So, too, in "If It Would All Please Hurry" (*CD*, 39), the speaker begins the narrative by going inside to go to sleep, to be alone: "I do not wish / to share the cliffs with anyone." He feels a loneliness, then imagines an other: "I feel you are in it [the bed] too." The poem is an attempt "to get into the habit of realizing you are real" and ends with a prayer — as if reality and realization could be made coincident: "*Hold tight, squeeze*." This sort of process — making the self by expanding the realm of the moment, goes on endlessly; the end is forever deferred, the poems deny simple closure. So, Tate says in "If You Would Disappear At Sea," an earlier poem — "the door is everywhere and yet, / parenthetical, thankless; / so close to home, no way to get there."

III

The Alien Sky, The Irrisistible Hearsay

"Look back, what life has become: the sky / is clearly alien, amazement, / star of my night blasts the subtle shifts / of mood," the speaker exclaims in "Heatstroke" (*RD*, 4). What the poet does within the predicament I have been describing is to become a mythologizer of the imagination. The woman described in "Heatstroke," for instance, becomes a "myth squeezing itself," the product of "need." Any dismantling, as we saw earlier, is also a process of reconstruction, of myth-making: — "tear them down / and build them up — it's one motion." It is from this impulse that poems like the mock romance "Missionwork" (*RD*, 59) emerges. This poem, a prose poem in ten parts, concerns Klingbat, a captain and several others in a parody of Conrad's "Heart of Darkness," a parody that leaves the central and disturbing issues intact. And this mythic impulse is the source of a poem like "Riven Doggeries" (3) which dramatizes loss comically and grotesquely (a dog has leapt, not been abducted by a police helicopter from a 7th story window), and just as tongue-in-cheek reconstitutes a mythic creature — "the ideal pet, however, / is unrecognizable when it arrives / in the river awash in the land afar." Riven — river — revive; doggeries — doggerel — dog; — the poem's myth originates in the play of language itself, a language of loss and diminishment, not an outside source. The poems become as Tate suggests in "Spring Was Beginning To Be Born" (*CD*, 18) "disguises," "murmurs," "splutterings," bits of language coming together:

> Spring was truly begging to be born
> like a cipher that aspires to the number one.
> Hush. It is all hearsay, irresistible hearsay.

To ignore the hearsay in speech — the overplus of language — is to deny the self, or as Tate says, to be "erasing my hearsay and stifling my double."

In this way (hearsay), a poem like "Wild Cheese" (*CD*, 15) becomes a sort of Popa-like myth about a cheese-like person or person-like cheese; the poem originates, really, from the scrap of colloquial language that ends the poem: "That certainly was a wild cheese!" A poem like "Constant Defender" (33), on the other hand, does not originate in a single saying but accumulates a sequence of improbable sayings ("The thing I'm trying to avoid is talking to my mule about glue futures"), often parodic ("this too, too static air"), often concerning absences ("In a rush to meet my angel, now / I don't even know who my angel was"). The result is a mythic world predicated on diminishments — "every meatball's burial" (literal and figurative), "this sluggish pit of extinct sweet potatoes" — but diminishments that reveal, by their quasi-mythic attachments to death and extinction, the seriousness of the speaker's predicament which he tries to hide, even from himself. So the poem ends comically, but touched in the last line by melancholy:

> Last night a clam fell from the stars:
> a festive, if slippery occasion, a vibrating blob
> entered our midst — I say "ours" out of some need —
> I was alone when it hit me.

And in "To Fuzzy" (*CD*, 47), a sort-of seduction poem set against a backdrop of Pharaohs, thaumaturgy, the Nile, and other exotic contexts, the speaker reveals a dream that admits his own predicament as writer:

> I would be reading a letter,
> written in Chinese calligraphy, in pencil, scribbled hastily,
> and its central motif would be the mat the author was sitting on
>
> and the writing pencil with which his hand and arm, torso and brain
> and a lifetime of witnessing, were struggling, I know there are
> contradictions in all I say. Fuzzy, whence is the unseen
> vindicated?

It is the unseen, then, that holds the fragments together — like the cipher —, that needs to be unravelled in language, that necessitates the mythic vision, that suggests the undercutting of simple visual images, of simple presences, moments.

"Tragedy's Greatest Hits" (*CD*, 59) perhaps best summarizes the tone and process I have been describing. Even the title undercuts the surface meaning, allowing the speaker a certain distance, detachment, a spaciousness from which to speak, "stutter," uncertainly. Near the beginning, the combination of "puddles and tensions," and then the mention of "cruel boats" produces a somber, though further undercut, tone. And yet, in the next few lines when the speaker mentions "floating" and "barking fetters" in the same breath, the pun on "bark" as animal sound and boat explodes the tension completely, denying the poem's other senses of doom, fate and confinement. From this perspective the speaker can both share in a tragic mood and counter it with a questioning of its stasis. This is the stance Tate deploys at his strongest, which is indeed quite strong in these poems, a stance which sees the self always in relation to its changing histories, that accepts its limits while expressing in its language an uncanny freedom, an intense and yet muted desire:

I was the stuttering monster who accepted
his doom. But he was coasting
on the past.

Life moves on, where are the miracles?

It's twelve o'clock, I wish
it were eleven fifty-nine.

Ralph Angel

You Are The Place You Cannot Move

You wake up healthy
but you don't feel right. Now everything's
backwards and you're thinking of someone to blame.

And you do, you're lucky,
drinking coffee was easy, the traffic's
moving along, you're like
everyone else just trying to get through the day
and the place you're dreaming of seems possible —
somewhere to get to.

All you really know
is that it hurts here, the way feelings
are bigger than we are, and a woman's face
in a third-story window, her limp hair
and the pots of red geraniums luring you
into her suffering until you're walking on roads
inscribed in your own body. The maps
you never speak of. Intersections, train stations,
roadside benches, the names of places and
people you've known all bearing the weight
of cashing a check or your having to eat something,
of glimpsing the newspaper's ghoulish headlines.

Like everyone else, you think,
the struggle is toward a better time, though
no pressure surrounds the house you were born in.
Cool, quieter, a vast primitive light
where nothing happens but the sound

of your sole self breathing.
And you've decisions to make. Isn't that why
you've come? with a bald-headed man at the bar
and your friends all over the place, anxious,
tired, a little less sturdy than you'd hoped for
and needing someone to kick around, someone to love.

Committing Sideways

This might hurt a bit, stabbing away at conversation
when we could be quiet or snoring, I mean
waking up sick is tomorrow's business; (we like to say
that it wears our clothes). But what's substantial
is the soulful intersection of the needs and obligations
of good friends ridiculing each other. It's a chance

we don't hesitate to take, and we're a shambles,
aren't we? These arms don't work anymore. Better stack
    them
over here, where the suntans fell off our faces. And yes,
that's the old philodendron walking out in your slippers,
but forget it, it's nothing, the whole place and its aura
of lived-in azaleas are resting on tentative sands.

Funny little murmurs of free fall. Now we're
getting somewhere, so close and, therefore, so disappointed,
like slap-happy derelicts leaning on parking meters
after the shoppers have thinned away, and yet from them
emanates an excited kind of trust that can also turn inside-
    out
and make visible what has remained so secret.

And we each say, "Well, here's to you, Bub," as the last
jokes collide with the things we most
despise in ourselves, which march across the table like
    crummy
peanut butter sandwiches in day-glo trenchcoats—whoops,
there they go—right through the breathy curtains,
right past the worry that we may be anything but

deadly serious when they return to us, as they always do,
when we're alone, and that our having to think about them
will hold us too safe and too separate, our feet
squarely planted in dreaded plots of ground.

Michael Augustin

A Terrible Disappointment

Koslowski has been, as far back as he can remember, utterly convinced thay he would one day be one of the three best violinists in Europe. But when, at the age of 36, he held a violin in his hands for the first time, he, as he told his friends confidentially, "almost broke out in tears," he was so disappointed by the design of this instrument, which he had —to use his words—always pictured "at least three times as large and somehow with corners."

Exaggerated Consequence

Koslowski tends towards exaggerated consequences. Since, for example, being shot at by British dive bombers during World War Two because of a highly visible brilliant red knit hat, he hates all knit hats, no matter what their color.

Sleepwalking

For a while it happened that Koslowski, a notorious sleepwalker, would leave his bed every night, wander through the harbor areas, return somehow, and in any case wake up utterly filthy in the cellar on a pile of coal and briquettes. In order to out-smart himself, so to speak, Koslowski has lately taken to lying down on the pile of coal and briquettes in the cellar at bedtime, and then he wanders, as always, through the harbor areas, and wakes up in bed. Still utterly filthy — but still.

Self-Portrait

Koslowski, decades ago, glued a photo of himself, the only one which exists, by the way, over the mirror in his bathroom, the only mirror in his apartment. Since that day he has painstakenly avoided ever looking into another mirror. Because of this, Koslowski today has only a vague idea of what he looks like, an idea, as he admitted not long ago, which "may be flattering, but which is, without a doubt, not a reverse image."

Immaculatus

Koslowski belongs to that tiny group of people who came into being through immaculate conception. "Whether in my case too the Holy Spirit had a hand in it, or perhaps even God in Heaven, I just don't know," Koslowski mentioned to friends. In any case when he was younger and slept with his natural mother for the first time, he claims that he found out that she was without a doubt still a virgin. A story, though, that hardly anyone accepts. "Afterwards," Koslowski notes with resignation, "afterwards, something like that is pretty damned hard to prove."

An Excellent Sentence

One morning, as Koslowski awoke, an excellent sentence immediately occured to him which he would not be able to rid himself of until the noon hours. "It was so humid and oppressive, it felt as if the air was running a fever." A sentence which just about any novelist would surely lust after. In the course of the morning, Koslowski used just about every available opportunity to make his sentence public, at the baker's for example, or with the fat but friendly lady in the meat section at the supermarket. In the tram, when Koslowski had just unleashed his sentence again, a gentleman interrupted his parade rather rudely: "Excuse me for a moment—but you're acting as if that were your sentence. It exists in Ödön von Horváth, Suhrkamp-Lesebuch Edition 1976, p. 44. I know that, I'm a German professor!" An embarrassing situation for Koslowski, because the gentleman was perfectly right. But he consoled himself with the fact that the whole day actually had been so humid and oppressive that the air felt like it was running a fever.

Tina Barr

North of Kennebunkport

The breakers had dredged a trough
along the water's edge, shelved stones,
the way they shelve sand
and a wader, stepping down,
stumbles and sinks to his waist.

Each stone was rolled round,
colored eggshell, ebony or brick,
white as bleached clam
or pink quartz ribboned green.

She hefted their palm-sized weights
as she lay level with the waves.
Looked up, saw into the clear
gelatinous belly of the wave —
transparent as a jellyfish around
its globular clover of red membrane —
Inside, green sea lettuce, rust dulse
rolled and floated.

Seeing that pull and draw
she remembered the way she had rested
her head on Michael's chest,
each muscle closing tight
as the black mussels that cleave down
locked together in the seabed's mud.

Waves broke their water
drove the periwinkles like marbles
and she heard the clack, clack
of stones beneath her, felt them shift
as the water drained back.

The shifting—sudden
the way she had felt
when she knocked on Michael's office door
and he held off too long
before he clicked the lock.
A girl sat in his chair
her head averted, his face
clean of expression, so earnest.

Public Garden Above the Rhone

In the public garden
that hangs in the air
above the Pont d'Avignon
behind the Palais des Papes,
where seven popes ruled from their fortress,
you hold my arm, while the wind,
the mistral, lifts the purse from my side,
my skirt above my thighs.
But here, no one looks
and if I hold your arm
two women, who touch,
no one turns their head to stare.

The german girl's skirt
rises and luffs in the wind
and a young man, bending his knees,
takes a picture
as she presses her skirt down.
The mountains, where Cezanne painted
the thrust of the earth's shoulder
creep up over her shoulder.

But what he cannot take
is a picture of the wind
as it shows itself
running like current
on the terraced lawn below,
as it lifts each sliver of grass,
makes troughs and gulleys.
And he cannot capture the comet trails
of its path, visible in the grass,
waves of heat sheening.

The wind shows us this,
some message, some image,
in the lawns of public gardens
in this country, where wisteria
grows in a museum courtyard
and I can gather
the weight of its blossoms
to my chest and inhale its scent.
In this country the lady
who runs the hotel smiles
and pleats the edge of a napkin at her table.

Donald Bell

Introduction of Dolphins

Blue animal
in a blue affluence,
silver-blue
ocean mammal

pointing in a green-blue
sea towards
a thin sparkle, the far
surf in the sun.

You're one with an intimate language:
the possible loneliness
of no-one-to-talk-to.

Swimming out, somersaulting
in the salt,
your destination:

lone dolphin, *X,* meet
fellow speaker, *Y.*

Imagine the Man

who carries wood across a virgin
half-acre of snow towards a door
in a house made of wood,
imagine his pleasure hearing the crunch
of each footstep, his boot
contrapuntal through a sub-freezing
patina. Also, his stronger
pleasure hearing the wind sing
an aria full of winter: *white,*
white, opera in a blizzard....
Around him trees whip and foam
dropping needles and nuts of snow
on mounds of snow. So
you can hear his pleasure,
can't you? He's pleased.
He stands at his window.
He lifts
his steaming cup,
and sips.

Michael Burkard

Star for a Glass

So many churches against the sky,
a small view beyond where a corner of the sea
converges with an even smaller landscape,
the spit less than motionless, as in a dream
where there's flame but not fire, where a child's cap
blows slowly across the street, where the land
ends where the street ends, and a man and a woman
turn their heads around.

Snowlight, a star for a glass.
I can still breathe. Although I have descended
too far into the April earth, I can still look up
and see the sky through the hole,
the one last snowfall in a light which must be
evening. To feed, to feed. To take your last name,
shout the name

— to walk out into nothing as the nighting is

Side with Stars

I bought gasoline and ink
(I did not buy booze,
I did not buy the moon,
I can no longer afford the moon).

But moon moon
what did you buy?
A mosquito with a net,
a plaything (air), a lantern
lit by gasoline for your other side,

side with stars, side by side
with streams, holes which breathe
like nostrils of solemn freight?

Saint. You purchased a saint.
A sun to correct
the dubious nature
of the saint's vibrating voice,

voice which adorns the emotion
with feelings from still
another side, the side

of fire stars, the fires burning,
the mosquito escaping
from the burning net,
clasped tenderly

in the palm of the saint.

Mornings like a Vase

No one holds my silent
mornings like a vase,
the card for unhappiness
represented by a single teardrop
hovering over the vase.
Aunt Vase, I call it, while Aunt Linda
focuses on the golden sun
as she centers my reading
for me. But what I remember
best is the snake in the grass,
pronounced as vase,
and who the hell could that be?
I know, I know, I'm concentrating
on the wrong image, because this image
is only the shadow of people,
and some other more ramifying card
is getting overlooked.
Shadow of a bicycle: now there's
a card: it represents a childlike
accident, or love broken late
in life, looking at pictures
of Anna and Jim. Or it means
the loveless shadow which
reflects a loving form.
I'll pay you 8 dollars
for this window of your former
life, a cold village on
the brink of spring.

The Family

I decided to never worry
again when I could not see the stone,
I decided the sky was there,
even in the skyless night
even when the family name

awoke and roamed. The family
name made so much noise! like the sea
which had buried some other blood
some other box of clothes
which washed up on the shore

like a misshapen house, the kind
a child would make, leave out in the rain,
later destroy. I decided never to worry
about this kind of house,
this kind of shore,

this kind of sea which bore
the family name among so many other
family names they might as well
have all been snow, truly, just being
family names accounted

and unaccounted for. I could not keep
the counting anymore. I could not look
and breathe at the same time unless
I became the breathing

of the shore or another name
which also roamed
by breathing. Maybe the stone
decided for me, or stone in my hand

we both decided. I can't tell.
I can tell it wasn't abstract anymore,
that it was finite

like the sun confronted by a thought,
which is finite because it is
a confrontation. I can tell

the family moved again, this time
without a name, for the names were done,
the house was done broken.

Pentimento

It will always be just love, spider failure,
curious, worn dead life, home in September,
far from all love. The radiant agent of
the breast is my express, my station of
pentimento, my erasure of the hemmed.
My sad dream when my eyes said I do not
love you, as good as we are.

In the unusual season the sun rises, harp
for a stone, starry glaze from the web
burned widely with paint. And thus and
thee, these two guarded friends, where
your dear love was a name.

Yes, but the bowl has no odor — and the agent
orange is the effort of a traveler,
poverty and stone, death's palate to kiss
the baby. All children government.
A spoon knows better, an ear.
Pentimento of little eggs, accept my
dead thus, my voracious female bullet.
Take heed when the wind calls — it may
be your uncle, smoking a cigar
in his death, whiff of smoke
doubled by the world. And looking
into the anger recall the octave
of the spoon, eat accordingly.

Follow me into the continual
death of the house, shelter for
a number. It is today my coat
is a dagger, bled — today

I cut the rope. Today I come back
to the night, full of sadness
and your letter. Today I buy a house
in my mind, and sleep there with
my children. Today I shower with you.
Today I submit to the interview, today.
Today I burn the bookcase, today.
Today I bury my head in the groove
of the poor, today my breast is so dry
it is intense. Today I tonight.
Today I yesterday. Today I mail these stamps
to the mule Jennifer. Today I am my
wicked aunt. Today I paint the vertical
sorrow of each mirror, each thenness,
each scale of the double government.
Today I film flour. Today I come back.
To your night. Today. Today.

Elena Karina Byrne

The Collector Calls

Gifts of garbage, rare junk sink
into the corners of each room. I circle
around the empty faces of dolls; doll legs,
doll heads and doll hands full of sand
litter the dark floor, each undusted shelf
edging masquerade of nature's giving-in: bottles
the color of black ice, tin cans tortured
from art, a cat's tooth caught in a bird's wing
above my head and far out of reach bare
uneven bones of a fish filed from order.
I turn and turn, he smiles
watching each guest move sideways like crabs
stranded in a tide too low. Everything
speaks for itself, unanswered, deliberately
inarticulate: bells, more bones, rubber and rock.
I feel unfamiliar, out
of place in this collector's museum somehow
making him more or less of a man.
This universe is unhinged, each object his
ubiquity: iron needle and bow, a closing smell
of wet wood, this unnatural axel, forever
his wheel turning and turning
against our circular sleep.

The Sound of Sheep Before Shearing

July is an insult
of heat. We have made it
this far,
to the highlands, takers
and spectators, to the edge
of this highway without animal gladness
or melancholy, without answer
or tool of comparison.
Above us, these
jeering mountains dizzy
in the mid-day light, haze above the bleak
occasion of shearing sheep.

What is this antedeluvian moan, this
furry hysteria in their voices, crowning
in unison toward a kind of blurred
heaven, one
to another crying out mouth to mouth,
each small and large body swaggering thick with wool
and grey dirt?
Then what maker's waiver have we signed here?
Over
to the sound of sheep
shaping our own tongues around
the desolate nouns of these distances,
these woolen fields and broken stitches
of water, that last move
within us about saying *go*
or nothing at all.

Richard Cecil

The Call

In religion class we argued
about the weather in heaven.
Was it always sunny?
or did it rain once
a century for contrast?
I said perfect meant perfect —
sky would always be cloudless,
the sun at meridian,
shining evenly
through translucent saints,
who, like a stained glass dome,
would project their colors —
martyr red, hermit
gray and virgin blue —
over heaven's weedless lawn.
But Sister Marie Therese
pointed out that grass
withers without rain,
that day requires night,
and summer, winter, etcetera.
Her theory was that heaven
looked like southern France —
not as in her slides,
colorless with age,
which she'd shown each fall for years,
but as in the landscapes
of a painter named Van Gogh.
She opened a yellow book
to a picture of the sun

outlining a twisted man
beside a twisted tree.
— In this painting called *Sowing,* he shows
the sun as it looks in heaven —
she said, and turned the page
to a picture of pinwheel lights —
and in this called *Starry Night,*
he shows us heaven at midnight.
I bent forward, straining
against my rigid desk
to see tormented cypresses,
writhing fields of wheat.
Then she turned the page
to a portrait of the artist,
whose pale blue eyes
stared from a greenish face.
— And this is the face of a saint —
she said, and passed the book.
When it came to me,
I stared at every plate,
amazed and horrified
at how, like Frankenstein,
this painter had animated
the corpse of his inventions
Even churches breathed,
and cut flowers in a glass
looked tortured as his face.
So when I turned the page
and read that he'd killed himself,
I felt relieved. — Sister,
I said, — he shot himself;
he's burning now in hell.
Be quiet! said the boy beside me.
I looked around and saw
that everyone was drawing;
while I had hogged the book,

the class had gone on to Art.
I asked the girl behind me
what the assignment was.
Draw paradise—she hissed.
I took out my crayons,
sharpened the red and green,
and started to draw stick trees
and tulips in a line.
But then I saw the teacher
advancing down my row
frowning at stiff pictures
of flowers, clouds, and angels.
So I swirled blunt yellow
through the limbs of my trees,
and slashed my dumb blue sky
with black wings for crows.
—What are these? she asked,
pointing at my birds.
Those are the black wings
of heaven's suicides—
I said. She smiled, and nodded,
and nailed my awful picture
to her bulletin board that week.
For though I couldn't draw,
I had injected madness
and death into paradise.
—Richard will be an artist—
she announced. I groaned
and rolled my eyes and grinned,
but the mirthless class just turned
toward me with flat expressions
which for the rest of my life
I've practiced trying to capture
in my black and whites of hell,
leaving yellow to Van Gogh,
and heaven to his crows.

Applications

Last night, when drunken cries and ugly music
poured from open windows of apartments,
and the street outside my door was echoing
with shouts of boys and girls in open cars,
I typed my application, cheerfully,
for a teaching job up in Alaska. Who cares
if night lasts half a year as long as cold
drives revellers inside, and freezing rain
makes every road impassible with ice.

This morning, by the feeble light of dawn,
as blue October sky turned solid gray
and sleety drizzle tapped against my pane,
I typed my application for Hawaii,
thinking of its warm and steady climate,
so temperate that everybody lived
in wall-less houses before high rise hotels.
Please consider me for your vacancy,
I typed. *I'm prepared to relocate.*

Tonight I comb the job list once again,
reading by unsteady fireplace light
of openings in Kansas and Nebraska,
where wind sweeps snow across the plains so fast
the boring vista from my downtown office
of avenues of leafless cottonwoods
would change into a view of urban tundra
in minutes, stranding us delighted workers,
who'd shimmer in our candle-lighted windows.

And this year there's a job in Baton Rouge
for someone who is willing to take charge.
Although I've never had command of others,
I think that I could count experience
as guerilla leader of my one-man army,
ordering myself across the map
from position to position, never entrenching,
always falling back. I've lead myself
through darkness deeper than their cypress swamp,

and I'd lead them in such wide curves they'd think
that they were making progress, not just circling,
like those migrants in Siberia,
who cross their tracks just once or twice a lifetime,
having, in the interim, forgotten
the dismal landscape of their starting point.
I'd be like the chief who thrusts the flagpole
into its old hole on Main Street, sighing,
while his excited band takes in the view.

Why not just settle for this vacancy I fill?
I'd just decided to be satisfied
this evening, when an awful crash made me look up.
I saw a car beneath a shattered streetlight,
jammed against a tree, wheels spinning,
and ran out my door to help the driver.
But the rescue squad already had arrived.
I stood in rain, among the tipsy watchers,
and felt torn bark, and wondered—should I go or stay?
End like the manic car, or the tree it wounded?

Gillian Conoley

Some Gangster Pain

Eunice is tired of pain, everyone else's.
She wants some gangster pain,
to strut her thick ivories
in a collision of dreams, the pajamas-to-work
dream, the magnolia siege dream.

What ya got there. Eunice, say Johnny and the boys.
Eunice lives behind the bus,
another fleeing place,
riot of exhaust. She doesn't
have much to say,
but she says it, hello.

When the boys talk
she feels the mole on her cheek
shift to the corner she took.
She sees them snap their fingers
to no dog. She knows

they wouldn't understand.
She knows her feet point themselves forward
but she keeps walking backwards in rain,
her heels too fast, or the rain seeps
into trees, she can't tell. She likes this street.

Johnny and the boys got on
jackets that twitch.
Eunice wears a lot of accessories. The boys
paint a circle on the wall
the color of lips.

Alias

In sunglasses like dark lakes
I like the way
the car capsules me from conversation,
the smell of the day burning.

I write home, "Wind
through the door is in any house,
land from a window a hard pie."

It was a good house.
Shutters, soup. One day
in the mailbox the face
on the cover was mine, my eyes
in repose, the children unborn.

Clouds collect
in an endless shampoo, the road
before me definite, divine,
shimmering like emulsion. Limousines
carry dark cartons.

In the next town the parade
is always coming, batons
thrashing spoons. Motel
carpets roll out
like tongues.

I take off my many coats.
They hang
themselves. All over
the block are neighbors
calling my new name.

Della Cyrus

Mirage

How can I believe
   that once
I lived
   in the dark pool
of my mother,
   now ashes?

Or that these
   radiant beings
my daughters.
   now mothers,
unfolded
   from me?

Or that
   we all will
at last
   enfold
in the body
   of the earth?

I play it
   over and over
but
   like the atom
for
   the physicist

the seen and
the unseen
nod
at each other
on their way
in and out.

Gone

This black hole is empty
not just of eyes, voice, hands,
but of the least stirring
in the air.

It is a cave
so dark and still
there is not
the slightest flutter
of even one
bat's wing.

River Trip

Riding down the shallow rocky Sheepscot
the trick is to stay centered
on the rubber raft.
You have to watch out for crazy currents
that will hang you up
on hairy boulders.

Falling off is not the problem—
it's the getting back on
with the rear end of the raft
swinging away
like a
slippery fish.

You try to keep your eye out
for the clear chance and
you make frantic last minute choices
to go right—
or left—
only to nose into the bank.

But the hemlocks and cardinal flowers
don't get you where you're going
nor the easy minnows
in the shallow pools,
so you push off again
for midstream.

Where are the others?
Your neck aches
from looking ahead
and the pace is too fast

when you aren't snarled up
in river weed.

But here, now,
as you near the mouth
leading to the sea
the way calms down and widens out.
You can put your face on your arms
and float.

Stuart Dischell

Penny Serenade

I would walk
The snowy miles
To your house,
Not quite as far
As presidents
In legends walk
To go to school;
Nonetheless,
Something was
School-marmish
About you
Who had never heard
The names of certain
Sports figures,
Television actors,
Popular singers,
Famous race horses.
And I was not surprised
To learn that as a girl
You studied violin,
Attended Hebrew School.
School and religion
Meant little to me.
I threw a ball
Against the front steps
Or played out the roles
Of movies I'd seen.
There are no pictures,
And we made no children.

As lovers we were careful
To cover our tracks.
There's no proving
You and me.

At the Summit

Sharing spice cake and green tea,
Around the round table
In the walled garden,
The man with the thick black hair
And the seated women in blue
Have something in common.

It's not the rings on their fingers
Or the gold in their teeth,
Or that they share the same flatwear
And plates of bone design.

(though on any other day
it could be all of these.)

Zeus and Hera recline on couches.
The world's a stirred pot.
They bet and the innocents fall.
The crops get plowed under.
Clear winners and losers then,
And omens to believe.

Though the empires were corrupt,
The world had its beasts to name.
Continents brooded on horizons.
Stars were for telling fortunes.

Things went wrong but more slowly
Those days before the wind caught fire.

To the man with the thick black hair
And the seated woman in blue,
Sharing spice cake and green tea
Around the round table
In the walled garden,
Death cannot come in.

And they talk until the end.

Interstates

I took for the dawn
The steelmills of Gary
Burning their corner of the night.
But I was wrong. Dead wrong.
At four am the sky takes on
These willful transformations.
To keep awake, I sing off-key
The fading staticky tunes,
A dj's voice a thousand miles near.
My life has never been more
In my hands. An eighteen wheeler
Passes so close and fast
I can taste the cigar wedged
In the driver's mouth. Another
Brother rides headlong in the dark.
And what could he be thinking,
Driving so recklessly, I thought,
Thinking for us both. A woman
Asleep at the end of the road.
The usual concerns, and my own.
The green tint on the dashboard
Lit the little numbered dials.
I wish my days could be counted
As easy and clear. Figures of speech:
Machines quit and machines die.
And milestones are really important
If you want to get where you're going.
I couldn't care less.
I couldn't care more.
Hands on the wheel, wheels on the road,
I'm putting a few things together.

Fish Pier

Thousands of codfish
Glitter in open
Cases. They look
So still on beds
Of ice, I tiptoe
Around them. Gutted,
Dead instruments,
They will not trill
The high or low
Seas again. They lie
Quiet as knives.
They, too, were feared
By their lessers,
Squid and mussels.
Still, these losses
move me little.
Tomorrow they'll be
Wrapped in the news
Of today's paper.
Events surface
At this very moment.
At every moment
Bad things happen.
Death leaves a corpse
And violence often
A reliable witness.
But good deeds and blessings
Are mostly manifestations,
Too abstract for me.
The fish had faith
In open water.

Stephen Dobyns

The Face in the Ceiling

A man comes home to find his wife in bed
with the milkman. They're really going at it.
The man yanks the milkman off by his heels
so his chin hits the floor. Then he gets his gun.
It looks like trouble for all concerned.
Why is modern life so complicated?
The wife and milkman scramble into their clothes.
The man makes them sit at the kitchen table,
takes all but one bullet out of the gun,
then spins the cylinder. We'll let fate decide,
he says. For the sake of symmetry, he gets their
mongrel dog and makes him sit at the table as well.
The dog is glad to oblige but fears the worst.
North, south, east, west, says the man, who's the one
that God likes best? He puts the gun to his head
and pulls the trigger. Click. Whew, what a relief.
Spinning the cylinder, he aims the gun at his wife.
North, south, east, west, he says and again pulls
the trigger. Another click. He spins the cylinder
and aims at the milkman. North, south, east, west.
A third click. He points the gun at the dog who is
scratching nervously at his collar. North, south,
east, west, who do you think God likes best?
The man pulls the trigger. Bang! He's killed the dog.
Good grief, says the wife, he was just a pup.
They look down at the sprawled body of the dog
and are so struck by the mean-spiritedness
of the world's tricks that they can do nothing
but go out for a pizza and something to drink.

When they have finished eating, the man says,
You take my wife home, I'm sorry I was selfish.
And the milkman says, No, you take her home,
I'm sorry I was greedy. And the wife says,
Let's all go home together. A little later
they are lying side by side on the double bed
completely dressed and shyly holding hands.
They stare up at the ceiling where they think
they see God's face in the ridges of shadow,
the swirls of plaster and paint. It looks like
the kid who first punched me in the nose,
says the husband. It looks like the fellow
who fired me from my first job, says the milkman.
And the wife remembers once as a child
a man who called her over to his car,
and opening the door she saw he was naked
from his waist down to his red sneakers.
What makes you think that God likes anyone?
asks the wife. Wide awake, the three of them
stare at the ceiling trying to define the kind
of face they find there until the sun comes up
and pushes away the shadow and then it no longer
matters whether the face is good or evil, generous
or small minded. So they get up, feeling sheepish,
and don't look at each other as they wash and
brush their teeth and drink a cup of coffee,
then go out and make their way in the world,
neither too badly nor too well as is the case
with compromises, sneaking along walls, dashing
across streets. You think it is nothing to risk
your life every day of the great struggle until
what you hold most precious is torn from you?
How loudly the traffic roars, how ferociously
the great machines bear down upon them
and how courageous it is for them to be there.

Pony Express

Some would have you think the Pony Express
is dead. Don't believe it. It's only waiting.
You know the letter you thought of writing
to that woman you once loved, the one describing
how you remembered her hair or hands or
the curve of her chin? That's the sort of letter
they now deal in, and if you wrote it,
they would show up to take it. These days
they like apologies, regrets, the letters
that begin: If only I had known then
what I know now—these aged men with their
aged ponies, playing cards and polishing
their saddles in the city's only livery
stable, waiting for someone's change of heart.
Take the example of the old clerk who lives
by himself in a cheap room. Forty years ago
he loved a woman and now he dreams of her face.
If only he wrote, Sometimes, I think of you;
sometimes, I still desire of you; sometimes,
I wish I could hear you laugh once again.
Then suddenly there would appear at the door
a frail old man with a gunfighter moustache,
cowboy hat and brandnew red and blue checkered
neckerchief. He'd take that letter and, oh,
he would ride. He'd gallop his old pony
across highways, expressways, railways,
even airport runways until at last he reached
the cottage of a bright cheeked old woman
who would read the letter with one hand pressed
to her heart as the sunset twinkled and
from somewhere came the twittering of violins.
But of course the old clerk won't write the letter,

and as the world gets colder, he gets smaller;
and as the world gets harder, he gets meaner.
At night he perches over his hot plate
watching the sun collapse behind the high rises,
while across the city a last Pony Express rider
sticks his head from the stable door to see what
final shenanigans the setting sun is up to.
Why is it, they both think, that some days the sun
just seems to flash out as if someone had snatched
up its last light and smashed it to the ground?

Spider Web

There are stories that unwind themselves as simply
as a ball of string. A man is on a plane between
New York and Denver. He sees his life
as moving along a straight line. Today here,
tomorrow there. The destination is not so
important as the progression itself. During lunch
he talks to the woman seated beside him.
She is from Baltimore, perhaps twenty years older.
It turns out she has had two children killed
by drunk drivers, two incidents fifteen
years apart. At first I wanted to die everyday,
she says, now I only want to die now and then.
Again and again, she tries to make her life
move forward in a straight line but it keeps
curving back to those two deaths, curves back
like a fishhook stuck through her gut. I guess
I'm lucky, she says, I have other children left.
They discuss books, horses; they talk about
different cities but each conversation keeps
returning to the fact of those deaths, as if
each conversation were a fall from a roof
and those two deaths were the ground itself—
a son and daughter, one five, one fourteen.
The plane lands, they separate. The man goes off
to his various meetings, but for several days
whenever he's at dinner or sitting around
in the evening, he says to whomever he is with,
You know, I met the saddest woman on the plane.
But he can't get it right, can't decide whether
she is sad or brave or what, can't describe
how the woman herself fought to keep the subject
straight, keep it from bending back to the fact

of the dead children, and then how she would
collapse and weep, then curse herself and
go at it again. After a week or so, the man
completes his work and returns home. Once more
he gathers up the threads of his life.
It's spring. The man works in his garden,
repairs all that is broken around his house.
He thinks of how a spider makes its web,
how the web is torn by people with brooms,
insects, rapacious birds; how the spider
rebuilds and rebuilds, until the wind
takes the web and flicks it
into heaven's blue and innocent immensity.

How To Like It

These are the first days of fall. The wind
at evening smells of roads still to be traveled,
while the sound of leaves blowing across the lawns
is like an unsettled feeling in the blood,
the desire to get in a car and just keep driving.
A man and a dog descend their front steps.
The dog says, Let's go downtown and get crazy drunk.
Let's tip over all the trash cans we can find.
This is how dogs deal with the prospect of change.
But in his sense of the season, the man is struck
by the oppressiveness of his past, how his memories
which were shifting and fluid have grown more solid
until it seems he can see remembered faces
caught up among the dark places in the trees.
The dog says, Let's pick up some girls and just
rip off their clothes. Let's dig holes everywhere.
Above his house, the man notices wisps of cloud
crossing the face of the moon. Like in a movie,
he says to himself, a movie about a person
leaving on a journey. He looks down the street
to the hills outside of town and finds the cut
where the road heads north. He thinks of driving
on that road and the dusty smell of the car
heater which hasn't been used since last winter.
The dog says, Let's go down to the diner and sniff
people's legs. Let's stuff ourselves on burgers.
In the man's mind, the road is empty and dark.
Pine trees press down to the edge of the shoulder
where the eyes of animals fixed in his headlights
shine like small cautions against the night.
Sometimes a trailer truck lit up like Christmas
roars past and his whole car briefly shakes.

The dog says, Let's go to sleep. Let's lie down
by the fire and put our tails over our noses.
But the man wants to drive all night, crossing
one state line after another and never stop
until the sun creeps into his rearview mirror.
Then he'll pull over and rest a while before
starting again, and at dusk he'll crest a hill
and there, filling a valley, will be the lights
of a city entirely new to him.
But the dog says, Let's just go back inside.
Let's not do anything tonight. So they
walk back up the sidewalk to the front steps.
How is it possible to want so many things
and still want nothing? The man wants to sleep
and wants to hit his head again and again
against a wall. Why is it all so difficult?
But the dog says, Let's go make a sandwich.
Let's make the tallest sandwich anyone's ever seen.
And that's what they do and that's where the man's
wife finds him, staring into the refrigerator
as if into the place where the answers are kept —
the ones telling why you get up in the morning
and how it is possible to sleep at night,
answers to what comes next and how to like it.

Freak

For Byron Burford

A child is born with a third eye smack
in the middle of his forehead. It's not
worth much. He can't see with it, can't
ogle with it, he can only blink with it.
But this is good enough to get him a job
in a freak show so he spends his youth
sitting in a chair blinking his third eye
while crowds of people fall back and gasp.
At first, he doesn't mind being an oddity,
but by the time he is thirty he's grown tired
of traveling and broods about the small town
where he grew up and how he'd like to have a farm.
Therefore, he takes the big step of having
his third eye surgically removed and returns
home and buys a piece of land. But right
from the start it's a mistake — the bank
cheats him on the mortgage, the tractor
salesman sells him a clunker of a tractor,
the hardware cheats him on the price of nails.
But even worse, he's gone from being an ugly
man with a third eye to being plain ugly —
the jerk who the world pokes in the back.
So he sells the farm and returns to the show.
Who wants to be invisible? Billing himself
as the man with the third eye and decked out
in his old spangled tights, he again sits
in a straight chair before people foolish
enough to spend a quarter to see some character
with a badly painted blue eye on his forehead.
What do you see? calls a joker at the barrier.

But the man with the third eye is too proud to answer.
He now understands the divisions of the world
and has made his choice and even a third eye
done with paint is better than no third eye at all.
As for what he can see, if he wanted
he could describe a field of white, let's say
a field of white flowers or snow or sand
with no tracks or interruptions, nothing to show
usage or the casual depredations of man.

Edison Dupree

None Other

Matthew 27.50,51

What can still bleed is not yet food.
In the ninth hour Jesus howled
and his wounds' crusts were opened. Blood
repainted its dried trails. He felt

the scourge's language on his back
burn for interpretation, final
insight, some emphatic look
into the memoirs of the Cruel,

the Other. But none came. His face
dilated, he seemed about to laugh,
then cried again with a loud voice.
The long veil ripped itself in half.

At Your Hanging

The hangman weeps. He kneels and begs
forgiveness of your shoes. OK,
OK, you nod, and your headbag's
spice, its tropical jute bouquet,
grows subtler, like some wine you are
adrift in. This the hangman frantically
understands, and everyone here,
in sunlight and authentically
ash-blackened sackcloth, deeply feels.
Now we lay us down to dream
those colorful cold subsoils
your face must crumble and become,
and now the hangman's drying his eyes
on the soft rag of the noose.

The Donation

The ten-car Interstate collision
has shucked me from the body.
My little heat ascends toward space,
and now, under the surgery theater
lights, they are lifting out my usable
parts to be reinstalled, to keep
some stranger going awhile.
Goodbye, old heart, old greased purple
fist. Keep slugging, just one more
inevitable rejection.
So long, kidneys, old beans.
Where you're going you'll find plenty
of work, plenty of dirty blood.
Look sharp now, eyes. I kept you dry
and open all those years, don't go
and cloud up on me now.
Honor our old bargain
with the sun. Remember the good pay
that came to us daily in gold and all
we had to do was wait, oh we waited
at high speed for that meeting.

A Life of Crime

If I should purchase necktie, hat and cane,
spats, and a natural shoulder double breast-
ed suit, and stroll downtown, would I attain
to Class? My heart is sinking in the west.
If birds above me, singing to enfilade
me top to bottom with sweet tracer fire,
lit up my brain's molecular arcade,
would meaning dawn? or beauty, or desire?
Most likely I'd just move along to work
for the Pinhole Condom Company all day;
come home destroyed; lie down, and feel the pork-
chop warmth of the radio preacher's voice: "Today,
friends, is the first day of the rest of your life!"
—each vowel glistening like a kitchen knife.

for John Vargas

To the Glistening Center of a Period,
On a Page of the Newspaper

O microscopic, ice-capped
summit of human eruptions,

under the high intensity
lamp your ink gleams diamond-

like, as though a stone your size
were precious individually,

whereas we know only en masse
is diamond dust useful,

e.g. sprayed up onto midnight
as constellations, animals,

heroes, queens, utensils,
about whom outsized stories

got told because night dragged, and the fire
cast shadows — as do stories now

that physics looks like ethics,
whose arguments, like history,

labor toward an end
you will not signal

Mary P. Fister

Cumbrian Herd

They dally on succulent
fields of ferment
while days pitch away.
Their jaws move in circles
like a woman's seasoned fingers
delving bins
at a rummage sale — both know
green's secret outposts
in dark corners. And
noses stroke the ground,
hothouse breath coaxing tubers
to curl up another year.

They have the privilege
of this valley.
Some curve their backs
to the trickling sun.
Some raise their heads
at a catcall in the breeze.
Hooves springing like warped boards
print routine's cleft procession in mud —
brimming udders soon
cluster, wobble between hocks
pull them barn-close.
Birds follow to moor on
grain in droppings.

They crowd the door,
saunter to stanchions, square hips
bow under white foam's load.
He works the line,
his hands knead teats
to each one's rhythmn, starts
the rumble of release. Mist skimmed
from buckets of hot milk
thickens on panes. By morning
mist will turn
into frosty plumed birds
who peck at sills,
setting them fieldward again.

Sounding

Already the leaden sky dissolves
and changes into a red-orange
plume on water—

as if our low-gear motor
mixes magnificent pigments
that funnel in,

then diffuse. And even though
we home in on a pocket
of river-must

where the anchor
will take hold, the sun
in our wake, that leavening

distance so slow
in coming gives a sense
of leaving for good.

From sea, some trees
spread flat as crewcuts,
others stoop under

the wind's greatcoat,
another straight as a girder,
(that singular ascension),

all on one shore!
So it's as courters
we float this slow

tidal feed, crouch
close as we can
to the soundless glint

of fireflies, a buoy's
undertones, and the nervous
peal from an osprey's nest

where the rev slows
and we drop anchor...
We spread an embroidered tablecloth

of mismatched threads
over the engine house
for our dinner

of sandwiches, cherries,
and wine. An entre-deux-mers
ever-sharpening by toasts

made to soothe the ospreys;
this odd coincidence
between name and

teetery locale.
Water-locked, we know
anywhere is possible

if we allow our eyes
to be lead by that keen
retriever slicing the water,

limp duck in his soft mouth,
as we once caught
each other off-guard,

pointing to one dim signal,
where we gathered
two castaway hearts.

Maria Flook

Memory

We are not mentioned by others,
never greeted by friends.
We return to a place and follow
a mystery to its little hole.
The sky had no imprint, it rained
the way ink drips off newspapers,
and we hid behind that year
as if behind a blank billboard.
Perhaps a cold observer
could have written an ending
to this, as tired journalists
identify faces in a burning building
and only the names are saved.
It was long ago and never recorded
on forms, a beautiful suspicion
with no official blame.
Even a girl, whispering the rules
of a game, was misunderstood.
Someone waves a flammable rag
in the same neighborhood
where some workers played a radio
so we could not hear of love,
that squeak of a pulley.
The world at night burned black,
a low inaudible voice, and its echo
the smoke.
Each day curled up like a curtain
on fire, as anything left too alone
becomes wrongdoing.

The Beautiful Illness

"Illness is a long lane..."
—John Keats

I can't forgive an old theme
in spring. Powdered aspirin
on the lips of white lillies,
the antiseptic color
injected in these lawns
reminds me of a beautiful illness
but I can't imagine coming down with it.
I'm out walking in a mood; it shames me
that six or seven gloomy moths,
my pet irrationalities,
and all my nervous thoughts are after me.
The evenings are warm and busy,
an atmosphere of crowded sewing rooms
where they make the lace attachments
for homely wedding gowns.
I think of love, how it should be drowned
like a spider in a drop of water.
A dull, reluctant drizzle would suffice.
Something falls in other lives
like footsteps coming
or someone kicks a tin can
tenderly all night.
A careful loitering might attune me
to my needs when the cheapest expectation
seems too dear. With this in mind,
I paid for the last newspaper
with its torn headline, to read of a place
where business was booming, but the faces
on money looked so dejected

I flattered a cashier
who was going off duty.
Of course I was joking, I left
in a flurry. A circle of insects
laughed along with me, convulsed
in precise, lonesome amusement.
I give up telling the truth to any stranger,
and I can't worry about women who knew me
when I was used as an example.
Last winter, pneumonia sent out love notes
to many. Now tulips ascend like fevers,
the dogwood solicits my sickest responses.
It's useless to blame this season
or the next, and I don't excuse my part in it —
The desires left stupified in public hospitals.
Why does it matter, for love evoked so easily
was lost, thank goodness, beyond memory.

The Past

They were laying tar on the streets today
and tar on the roofs. Then the night,
the unsightly stars like the pocked face
of somebody, and the face must be forgiven.
I sat down on the stones that are finished
and I looked at the clouds
that are not finished but moving on, somewhere.
I acted so lovesick.
I did not think about the past,
it thought of me.
Recollection infested the halls;
a spider planned an hour
around my dull activities.
Solitudes so slight can walk diagonally
across the wall, even the corner of my room
leaned away as if to find another home.
It's easier to forget the dead
than to forget the living; both sorts
ignored my nervous inquiries.
My intention was to start immediately
at something's end, a disappearance
so lovely I believed it was flirtation.
This unhappiness, its hands
that cannot sooth whatever particle
of God still infects me.

The Stone

I drive peculiar routes to come this way.
Just yesterday, I coasted near
to see the house accented by some candlelight
at dusk, the hour when foolish dinners
have begun. I didn't care.
Behind an unfamiliar fence, the grave
was there with all its morbid qualities
unchanged. Add to this an element of rain,
a perverse gloss
against the bare marble of one name.

Pumpkins rotted on those shoulders
every fall. A sullen stone,
in winter it was marker for the snow.
Children played near as if under
the strict guidance of a nun who taught
monotonous ciphers, the inventory *one*.
It cast a narrow shade across the lawn
like an isolated bed inside a sickroom.

How immaculate it seems, and wastefully
quiet as the night falls like a dollar
no one reaches for. From the window
of a room, someone disapproving pulls
a curtain. But memory insinuates so much
it leaves an impure touch upon the clearest thought.
Let each day sink here.

Whoever rests beneath that brutal word
was first to organize all punishments
and rules. As families imitate their needs
and the bones' white solitudes are formed,

our bratty loves and brotherhoods resume
their childlike strategies.
I'm still scolded by unhappy laughters
from that house, even now,
in the small committee rooms, in the city
which grows upwards to escape.

Alice Fulton

Works on Paper

A thrilling wilderness of bio-
morphic script, you said
my letters scared you. And it's even worse
in person: pink oil of lipprints, unnervingly organic
Hi's, those kisses like collusions. For a moment
we vibrate like underwater
stones. What is this
windfall? We are not
easily becalmed. How you pull back
as if to deflect affection. How I pull
back, swear
to work at blandness, clothe myself
in jokes. Graft the properties of bland

to the social handshake
and we'll have it: how to get through
this world intact. Placebos do
nicely—expressions never point
blank but fixed
like bets between grin and grimace.
What I work to know is whether passion,
roaring, snapping
its head, can be prelude
to entertainment, harmless as MGM's
old lion. And is seduction a science
or a pattern of cheap frills; can you make it
from a kit? What suave

impoverishments we chose.
And I can do it: fake
formality, dissemble
with the best, lady it
over lessers: Pick me!
Pick me! Of course not
to care, to keep
the heart complacent as a dumpling,
that's hard. What of emotions
that grow so steep they can't hold
shape and the pinnacle
leaps forward, breaking as it does
in waves. I'm afraid

those emotions keep us lonely.
I'm afraid there are no bribes
equal to the body-
guards. We love surface
articulation. And when we say
Abandon abandon we mean it
as a command. Here's an illustrative touch:

Delacroix, old realist, got so excited
entering a harem's room
he had to be calmed
down with sherbets. Passion! Maybe
it only works on paper. But once
in a well-lit room
I buried my face in the material,
shirting, that opened to darker emulsions, rich
scents unlike others as burnt umber's
unlike other colors. It was about expansion.
There were brief constellations
down the willing
nerves, an effulgence: worth it, worth it.

Fables From The Random

(To Hank)

As sun tugs earth into an orbit,
fattens apples to red
spheres, as darkness holds
the dyes in cloth or paint keeps
iron assets intact, you preserve, you make fables
from the random.
What breaks without changing

doesn't signify: a china cup
to china chips—that can be
fixed. But paper flaming
to something other
than paper or the yin-yang
commas in frogs' eggs growing
longer, unrestorable,
alarm the orderly,
the four-four pulse in you.

Threatened expressions settle
at the bottom of your face,
tempting me to chemistry, a science
that locates elements in order
to control them. My mind tips
at every quibble, a scale
capable of weighing hairs.
Have I discovered any comfort?

I learned burning
is a chemical change
and that I'd rather see

the trees take a powder, the sun
give me the slip
than see the last of you
and your insistent rejection
of what is
and shouldn't
be. Seeker of agendas
hid in astigmatic

mayhem, I need you.
When I tossed bouquets through the open
window of your high and empty room
some weedy flowers drifting
on the bed, some dangling
from the sill,
you returned to wonder
how I'd managed without a key—
the daisies were so sweetly placed.

On The Charms of Absentee Gardens

Let's say the residents had other engagements. They've gone
off playing flutes made from wingbones of the golden
eagle. They've ascended to the abalone heavens, and left
alone, we prettify the long ago.
Aren't gardens most fetching when nobody's home?
When you can track the sunflower's tambourine face
twirling toward the sun.

The Anasazi angled rocks to catch the solstice
sun and show it in the shape of ingots
on a spiral glyph. We need such leavings—
not to tell the seasons but to help us
imagine famine, fire, the drama of
abandonment. To help us see
catastrophe—as if the mesa
were the basal column of a bomb drop.

Some say remnants of the World
Trade Center will leave much to be desired.
But isn't that a ruin's purpose—to be less
than satisfactory, only partly-
knowable, far gone, not fully
lovely, changing each observer into architect?
To make posthistory wonder
what god needed a prosthesis
of compressed, freestanding steel. Monolith, a rock

band, fired igneous music through the bars
of Troy when I was seventeen. The dance floor was a weave
of tawny light, as if we'd spread a spectral
Navaho blanket. When the singer let me coil
wires into rings and figure eights

after the show, the bar enlarged
to Madison Square Garden.

This was home: where girlish aspirations grew
flat as babies' heads
strapped into cradleboards, and boys
watched their hearts
like sundials that must remain unmoved
to point to something
true. What navigating fools

we were! We hadn't learned
a stable earthly object
kept on the left as referent
will send a traveler spiraling
into it, or that fixing on a heavenly body is the trick
to covering ground. I learned of others' sojourns
in the realms of gold and such
knowledge made me odd. Like a fig
grown in a Ripple bottle, my presence caused perplexity.

Leaving meant commencement. Legend says an angel
        banished us
with a sword of flame, though rumor
claims the owners torched
our hangouts for insurance.
In any case, we preened with self-
congratulation, as though our origins were ruinous
accidents from which we'd walked away.

Fire fixes the magnetic alignment
of clay, and wooden beams remember
weather in their rings. But what Cortez will come
in search of tambourines and beads? We'd like a past
that won't decay with distance or yield
to interference. Failing that,

we want what we've abandoned
to wear: that is to crumble
and to last. We want a ruin: uselessness
permitted the luxury of occurrence.

When I returned, the shadow of a fire
escape — liquid, amenable
to every hive and crator —
embossed a devastation.
And foglamps, spiked and harsh,
bloomed like sunflowers crossed out with light.

Lucinda Grealy

Ferrying horses

This is only a short trip
but the horses don't know that
blindfolded beneath the deck.
They stand tense and steaming,
I know their eyes are walled and bright
beneath the cloth.
Their hard breathing is my asking
what should I do? and telling myself nothing.
The ship's horn, a sudden shift;
it doesn't take much to scare them
and the dropped glass thing that does
brings a sudden bolt, the grabbing
of an ear and my digging fingers in a neck.
The mare, a dun, drags me along
like everything I won't let go of.
My face is forced next to hers
and for fifty seconds my life
is the purple I see in her nostril.

When it's over we're topside in the sunlight
and the ship's mate keeps asking Trouble?,
but I'm still thinking of being a color,
how everything became so sharp, so different.
Sound is another name for fear to these animals,
just as this ship is his own heart
to the captain, and for the men
working on dock the days are rope
and the words nearly over.
On shore there's a woman whose life

is beneath her window each warm night,
a person's wanting her to forget everything
and come out. She's the shade of red
lonely women paint their walls.

Stories from the train

From the train among row after row
of empty buildings you see
a single curtained window,

an orange bottle on the sill,
and a small child's face
watching sparks from the tracks.

You can only start
to answer this after you've passed it,
when the train is already pulling

into another town where another child
is carrying a cardboard coffin
full of birds through the streets.

There is always a bird at everyone's window
but no one says a word, a finger
pressed beside the lips and the thumb

beneath the chin. Like the women
who listen to local superstition
and make bread each sabbath

telling the dough a lie as it rises,
then setting the loaves on the porch
as if the night were an animal

who'd steal them away, as if the child
were an animal who doesn't understand
the word no, you tell yourself no.

The woman you thought you knew on the corner
was really a stranger, the tapping you heard
was the storm driving jays and orioles

into the glass. Moments like this
you're not exactly sure which combination
of staircase, hallway, and face

most closely resembles your childhood.

Poem

For years I've been trying to remember my father
but strangely I can only recall him

as a woman in a red dress, though his picture
is still on the wall. His sadness was a long letter

in a drawer we never opened, my own sadness a door
that would swell and have to be shaken hard when it rained.

It rained so hard the day he died mother had to drive
even to the corner store. She thought the groceries

she bought that day would last us for years
and I remember best her sitting in silence for hours

with all that food while my sister and I
stood in the doorway holding jars of fireflies

we thought we'd rescued from the wet.
My sister and I loved each other when we weren't fighting,

I loved my mother when she wasn't silent, and we all
loved the rain even though it smeared the picture by the
     window

and left a fog so thick even the cows were getting lost.
I remember one bawling, a deep and expensive voice

pulling from the mud, heavier and heavier, a hand in my
     hair.
And I remember my sister losing her shoes in that mud.

We were both punished for this but it was alright
because when she stepped out of them the two holes

didn't seem empty, and the distance between them;
    accurate.

My brother

It's two am and I awake
feeling you've just left
some small diner. I imagine
wind swinging through
the door, voices closing
behind you. I remember
your last employer saying you've left
for he doesn't know where,
a woman in a motel
angrily waving an unpaid bill;
I've been content most of my life
with barely missing you.
When we do meet it always
seems a time we'd rather not.
With you drunk and angry,
the distance to our next meeting
is magnified by the words
you can't remember
in the morning, doors
that throb for moments
after being slammed.
How is it I think of you
now, in the dark?
Or when I see an empty bus depot,
or on the street, near dawn,
when I can pass a bar
at closing hour and hear
men talking loudly and emptily
of going home.

Something else

There's no moon
and it's a curse,

my heart beating slow
like a bad accident.

We're searching
for Bill's bird dog in the reeds

and it might as well be bones
I part with my hand, bending over

the long pale grass my eyes aching
like thin tails of light

the dory lamps leave on the river.
I find him first,

whimpering and full of mud.
I carry him to the truck,

the others behind me,
and think it's a long time

since I held something
in my arms this way.

In the kitchen
he lies near the stove

while we drink beer,
laugh about next week

and watch the first light
coming through the window

make the table something lonely,
without a home.

Jeffrey Gustavson

Palm Sunday

(Letter to Gary in St. Paul)

Silenter, emptier, never.
The sky's overcast, your weather's now mine.
I am troubled in a hundred places—
And contradicted, contradicted—
By the dull light.
                Polyphonic weather,
Eminentest mood-tinker, sensitivest
Most biological face of the physical
Globe, least durable, least endurable:
Accelerate my ascent and erosion,
Erode my nascent ascents, say no
A thousand times in a thousand thunders,
Mock me as the crow-mobs mocked Christ,
                       lave
My desert flesh as lavish Christ laved Levant,
O lavabo of the indifferent,
Laboratory of the attentive, God.

Easter Sunday

(Letter to Clyde Rykken)

Empty church, perplexingly uplifting
Morning. I swept the sanctuary twice;
Palm-spears, and the corn-silk nerve-threads palms spawn,
Eluded my diligentest brooming.
The sacristy will smell like a hay-loft
'til the end of Pentecost. The parish
(Shame! I resist the pun, 'pon my sexton's
Whisky oath. Shilling for the new grave!
Ah, damn shame) can perish for all o' me!
Unnatural. Immobility's not
My only style. I'll stroll to the river.
Still, I know there's not the remotest chance
I'll outwit, there or anywhere, my un-
Certainties.

Soon the ducks will return, will have returned.
They'll breed, breathe easily in the lengthening
Evenings, conquer idlers whether the idlers
Are in love with a sweet girl or not. Here
They met, here linked fingers, here lingered
And timidly kissed. Peter decided
To stop his Italian lessons, maybe.
They threatened to dilute his Greek, or so
He allowed himself, an *antico* self,
To suppose. "Do you live in Rome?" "Do you
Suppose peonies would be too declamatory
Next the gazebo?" Dilute his Greek! Is
Regret a prominent component
Of her gaze?

Christ Church, Cambridge
April 1982

Minnesota

Hesitate? The wide long river's
Extravagance
Decrees the boundaries of my insouciance, confides how
Little, how hourly less, it cares
For the parallel blunders of its
Parallel banks, twin antinomies,
Wind-wrinkled water's edgy lapping,
Mammered quibbles among pebbles,
Clishmaclaver, quaggy and wearisome
Thoughts of no stature,
Windlestraw, zilch-billows, death-
Blusters. Lord lift me above my days,
Scaffold or scuttle my skull, mind's hull,
Oxenesque tug

Nudging scarcely navigable barges
Cantankerous as ammonia
From midriver to the channel in
Front of the massive doors of the lock...
In February the grumbling booms
Cold nights of dynamite to keep ice
From cracking the Ford plant's power dam...
Mississippi's ice-scaly surface,
Chapped lips salved, sugary batture I
Walked timorously on two miles once
Before scaling the escarpment next
To the Breck School, whose church in flames I'd
Seen the fall before, walking restless.
Late one night.

Requiem Notes

I.

Strict eyes only for the naked sheet
I'll whip and goad to disloyalty
Then soothe to loyalty again
Before its day is out; lax eyes for all
Atoms else; no eyes for the unmeasured
Anatomy of the scrutinizing, male past.
                              *
My odds-sniffing, instinctively hesitant
Odd friend
Hamlet, my poor skeptical hamster,
First loved thing I looked on dead,
You once jawed aside your bird-cage's bars
And nosed down the cold air return
To the scratchy, egg-rack filter in the furnace.
Mom had a brain-storm and Pa found you there,
Shivering.

II.

Enough, magician; fold your cloak; give up.
The baby-spot's dusty beam died
Across the theatre's throat.
                              Many seconds later,
Blood and blood identical, they were still.
South of the abracadabra, south
Of the wand's wind,
Where chisels of ice quarry ice air —
They were still.
Will he lie in her arms forever,

A dead man with living flesh,
Pietâ,
Terrible conception?
I will play a saxophone in the wings.

Reine Hauser

Liquor

"...half-lit with whiskey"
— Seamus Heaney

half with wit and this
long night is illuminated
for its full many hours.

My friend is this bottle;
and my friend is raising
her glass. Here's to you,
bottle and friends, glowing

with the compassion adequate
liquor brings us. No work
tomorrow; and no one to say
morning has come. We're

fit for hours, we'll sleep tomorrow.
The sun'll climb over us
as the bottle depletes, slowly, for keeps.

Still Farther Away

(L.K.)

Can't you tell me when
or where you'll be here
or there, now and then?
Water laps at Crete
as you leave it, then turns around

Cape Cod as you land
on these American shores. On the Gulf
down here the sun
strikes me as Aegean—remember

the algae spreading on the pond
each year as spring developed
like a photograph, only greener
and greener? We cover water,

too; by plane or plain
contrariness. A move into motion
sets us each going: we leave and then
we turn and double back.
How I got to Texas was

through Tennesee last fall.
I skirted Memphis, Nashville,
every town not a highway.

The way I got in trouble
was by using a map,
following those lines
someone else laid out. I miss

everything I can't see
at 60 miles per hour.
Lawrence, I'm south
now, and I'm sorry.

Dill

Here is dill
and its sweet scent rising off the peas
steaming in their white bowl.
This is the language of fiction,
a picture shaped with our wits,
an energy that asks our hands to cup water
from the cold faucet, to wash children,
to do the tasks we set for them.

Here's another story which calls itself
by names I can hardly pronounce
or understand: the palpable language
of the natural and unnatural sciences:
uranium oxide, choloracetaphenone.

Choose a word to stand in for torture;
find notations to equal hunger
and terror. Here are words
which spell the destruction of our kind
from this place *earth* or any other:
nucleo—; neuro—; thermo—; chemo—;.

Still the white bowl sits calmly
on the blue tablecloth, releasing
its aroma into the air. We name the colors:
blue, white, green. Now tell me the words
which carry the full weight of love
and pure emotion. What power is this
which brings such abundance into our lives?

Marie Howe

Part of Eve's Discussion

It was like the moment when a bird decides not to eat from your hand, and flies, just before its flies, the moment the rivers seem to still and stop, because a storm is coming, when there is no storm, as when a hundred starlings lift and bank together before they wheel and drop, very much like the moment, when driving on bad ice, it occurs to you, your car could spin, just before it slowly begins to spin, like the moment just before you forgot what it was you were about to say. It was like that. And after that, it was still like that, only all the time.

After the Flood

(For F.W.)

You have decided to live. This is your fifth
day living. Hard to sleep. Harder

to eat, the food thick on your tongue,
as I watch you, my own mouth moving.

Is this how they felt after the flood? The floor
a mess, the garden ruined,

the animals insufferable, cooped up so long?
So much work to be done.

The sodden dresses. Houses to be built.
Wood to be dried and driven and stacked. Nails!

The muddy roses. So much muck about. Hard walking.
And still, a steady drizzle,

the sun like a morning moon, and all of them
grumpy

and looking at each other in that new way.
We walk together, slowly, on this

your fifth day, and you, occasionally, glimmer,
with a light I've never seen before.

It frightens me, this new muscle in you, flexing.
I had the crutches ready! The soup simmering.

But now, it is as we thought.
Can we endure the rain, finally stopped?

The Meadow

As we walk into words that have waited for us to enter them,
so the meadow, muddy with dreams, is gathering itself
together,

and trying, with difficulty, to remember how to make
wildflowers.
Imperceptibly heaving with the old impatience, it knows

for certain, that two horses walk upon it, weary of hay.
The horses, sway-backed and self important, cannot design

how the small white pony mysteriously escapes the fence
every day.
This is the miracle just beyond their heavy headed grasp,

and they turn from his nuzzling with irritation. Everything
is crying out. Two crows, rising from the hill, fight

and caw-cry in mid-flight, then fall and light on the
meadow grass
bewildered by their weight. A dozen wasps drone

tiny prop planes, sputtering into a field the farmer has not
plowed
and what I thought was a phone turned down and ringing

is the knock of a woodpecker for food or warning, I can't say.
I want to add my cry to those who would speak for the
sound alone.

But in this world, where something is always listening,
even murmuring has meaning, as in the next room, you
    moan in your sleep,

turning into late morning. My love, this might be all we
    know
of forgiveness. This small time when you can forget what
    you are.

There will come a day when the meadow will think
    suddenly, *water,*
root, blossom , through no fault of its own. And the horses

will lie down in daisies and clover. Bedeviled, human,
your plight in waking is to choose from the words that
    even now

thicken your tongue, and to know that tangled among them
and terribly new is the sentence that could change your life.

From Nowhere

I think the sea is a useless teacher, pitching and falling
no matter the weather, when our lives are rather lakes

unlocking in a constant and bewildering spring. Listen,
a day comes, when you say what all winter

I've been meaning to ask, and a crack booms and echoes
where ice had seemed solid, scattering ducks

and scaring us half to death. In Vermont, you dreamed
from the crown of a hill and across a ravine,

you saw lights so familiar they might have been ours,
shining back from the future.

And waking, you walked there, to the real place,
and when you saw only trees, came back bleak

with a foreknowledge we had both come to believe in.
But this morning, a kind day has descended, from nowhere,

and making coffee in the usual way, measuring grounds
with the wooden spoon, I remembered,

this is how things happen, cup by cup, familiar gesture
after gesture, what else can we know of safety

or of fruitfulness? We walk with mincing steps within
a thaw as slow as February, wading through currents

that surprise us with their sudden warmth. Remember,
last week you woke still whistling for a bird

that had miraculously escaped its cage, and look, today
a swallow has come to settle behind this rented rain gutter,

gripping a twig twice his size in his beak, staggering
under its weight, so delicately, so precariously, it seems

from here, holding all he knows of hope in his mouth.

Richard Jackson

Worlds Apart

I can't help but believe the killdeer,
so deftly has it led me,
dragging its own wings away from a poorly
hidden nest before clenching back into flight,
and I can't help but believe in a love
that would make itself so vulnerable for its young.

It is hard to understand, but
only by leaving do we know what we love.

Before I left, you told the story
of the fledging cuckoo who hatches in a sparrow's
nest, who spills out the native fledgings,
and is adopted by the vulnerable parents.
One night, in a city far from home,
I watched in amazement as two young men
who seemed more fierce than the cuckoo,
stooped to kiss some bag lady on the forehead
and pass her a dollar, a lady who had nested on a corner
with her dozen sacks and a cart.

Never have I felt so guilty
for what little love I could show.
That night, alone on a bus, I thought
you were the starlight nesting in the trees
that held every moment that had happened in your life.

In the pine woods along the coast north of here
starlight never touches the ground.
Somewhere in there the cuckoo will begin to sing.
I don't think there was ever a time we weren't
approaching each other through those woods.
I don't think there is a moment we have
that is not taking place somewhere else,
or a love that doesn't lead us, sometimes
deftly, further from ourselves.

For the Nameless Man at the Nursing Home Near the Shawsheen River

"You can't step into the same river twice"
—Heraclitus

Sometimes you step into a river twice
and it's the same river. The sky leans
down just to show the importance of sky,
Boys on the bridge are throwing rocks,
carelessly, at elusive carp in that changeless river.
They do not think of the love they have never known.

I have read somewhere that each pail of river
water holds nearly invisible worlds of life—
larvae, rotifers, algae, plankton, sponges,
diatoms, protozoa, seed shrimp.
It's as if each thing we have is another thing,
each moment we have, another moment.

There's no telling all this
to the old man smoking his white clay pipe,
its stem so long he has to keep his hand
extended as if to offer or accept a gift.
He is telling the best lies that will make
sense of his past that seems much longer
than his own life—one son's final letter
inventing a fragile world from some jungle,
another son's absent letters stuffing his pockets.
He is slipping into the river he wanted love to be.

I am not going to tell him
some allegory to bring him back to this moment
by pointing to the praying mantis on the railing
mounted by her mate from behind, turning
a shoulder to clutch it around the neck,
devouring its head even as they continue.
There's no sense telling him
that her mate's protein is what sustains her,
or to try imagining it knows all this beforehand.

I am just going to sit here with
this old man I hardly know, but who I am
going to say is my own father
whom I have denied long enough, the terrible
secret of sons, because it is true that
to fill the spaces between steps with love is
to empty yourself, to become the perfect lie
giving back the gift of emptiness, the perfect
emptiness of the river which holds everything,
what the boys know, — that there is
almost nothing that does not mean love,
however elusive, and that the loves we abandon
and the loves we keep are the same love.

Mary Karr

Moving Days

Folding the old monopoly board
I straighten the piss-yellow $500 bills.
If this were real . . . we thought as kids.

That sense of possibility is gone
though artifacts remain: the dirty string
that knotted charms — flat iron, silver shoe,

the choo-choo I might have ridden
anywhere. These rest in a junkyard sofa
or twinkle in the belly of the fish

we tilted down the toilet bowl.
And the great chain of command
yanks another notch, and I pack

this year's books for next year's
crackerbox, where I'll stand at the door,
glancing down the green road.

Like the woman I dreamed
on the step of my sturdy Boardwalk house
I'll kiss my hopeful pinstriped man

and listen for the thunder of the dice.

Home During A Tropical Snowstorm
I Feed My Father Lunch

1.
It angers me: the cold snap and freak ice storm
that's wrecked my yearly pilgrimage home.
Coming far from my northern province, I miss
the perfume of the cape jasmine,
and I want to smash the hard mush of tomatoes
in paint cans on the porch against the white house
and axe the crackling trees.
Such burden on the earth: no electricity,
no phone, just this glass coat that prevents
my really seeing, really feeling anything —
iced magnolia blossoms, bananas sagging
like gold ingots from the weight.

It's like the repression my father practiced,
who draped a dishtowel on his shaving mirror
against vanity, his tough Indian face
too beautiful. *What you can't see*
won't hurt, he said, and meant it
modestly and worked in every weather —
tropical heat waves, hurricanes.
He trusted the natural order of things,
which means he rests today on a soiled bed sheet,
an inch-deep sore carving itself
into his butt. And it takes an infinity
to spoon beef stew into his vacant face.
You might have studied yourself,
Father, whose portrait
on the empty spoon's silver I resemble:
long-faced, mouth stretched into a yowl.

2.
When he gasps and chokes blue on the fibrous meat,
a full space bar strikes in my chest
as I review the oath I made the doctor take
not to jolt his heart nor ever to notch
the windpipe for an automatic lung.
And that night I unwrapped the army-issue pistol
from his tangled socks and underwear,
cleaned it with mechanical oil he kept
and sat on the porch weighing
its male bulk and simplicity:
the crossed hairs like a plus sign
on the frozen orange moon,
but though glands in my throat
soured with the wish,
I could not invite his death,
and when he choked
I pried the leather jaw open,
poked my finger past the slick gums
to scoop an air passage
till he bit down hard and glared,
an animal dignity
glowing in his bird black eyes
which carried me past pity
for once, for once
all that terror twisting into joy.

Lindsay Knowlton

Central Park

Ignoring your poor prognosis,
we set grief aside and at dusk
behind the Met climbed
slowly towards the obelisk
where, resting a while, we might
in time's pinched frame
lavishly survey spring's blossoming.

You were so eager for smell—
nose in the first bloom at hand—
like the hummingbird
with his shrewd apparatus
you drank deep, and I saw that facts
were chaff,
that in perishing's lone
distillery
exactitude drifts
like a petal. To get it fast,

if you had to graft syringa's
sweetness
to scentless magnolia,
who could object? Not me,
—not the tree.

Gardenia

The night my sister wiggled
into her black sheath
and shielded her first corsage,
I took a deep breath
and learned about love:
how sweet the flower,
how the delicate blossom would bruise.
I don't remember the boy's name,
if my sister had a good time,
only a new kind of sadness
that was all my fault. After
she folded up her nylons and stopped talking,
I stole downstairs and slid the cellophane box
out of the refrigerator drawer.
For what must have been a long time,
I huddled on the cold floor,
undone by the satin magic:
if my breathing could turn
an ivory petal brown,
by touching, what I might kill.

Stuffed Rabbit

It's last call when a man you've met
asks if you'd like a black russian.
All night, he's talked sports and half-
listened to you. Still—he has
a lean body and luxurious beard and you
like lean bodies and luxurious beards.
So you nod and take little sips
of vodka and kahlua.

Sandwiched in a cab, you begin to feel
dizzy and think you may have
a change of heart, but the man is already
rubbing your thigh, whispering for you
to just relax. You wish you were somewhere else—
your first trip to New York: the toy store
when you headed straight for the rabbit—
its bright eyes, the satin ribbon holding
the bell: how, stroking its fur,
you couldn't bring yourself to quite let go.

On the way back, you clutched the rabbit
in your pocket, wanting to cry,
dying to tell. Now, as if you'd lost
any say in the matter, you bite your lip,
and feel someone else's fingers
dig into the fur, tighten on the bell.

Yusef Komunyakaa

Born Pretty in a Poor Country

Tuned for the big spenders.
Hardly an unbroken bone
in your body. Now you know
why your mama wanted
to give you just one kind scar
in the right place.
You're in these snapshots
dancing the cha-cha,
doing the dog with a sailor
from Chattanooga. The good life
poured from a green bottle,
a cigar smoker named Roberto
leaning in the doorway
said your name.
He cocked his hat
& you were twirling
under the corpse-maker's spotlight.
Before you learned his tune,
before the first bone
settled into its meaning,
flesh & dream fell away.
What's left those long nights,
doubled over to let life
go at you?

Flashback

A funny thing happened last night,
Betty-Lou. We were out celebrating
Willie's promotion at the plant,
having a grand old time. Candlelight,
champagne, roses, a hundred-dollar
dinner at The Palace. You won't
believe how fast it came over him.
A finger snap. A cornered look
on his face when a Vietnamese waitress
walked over to our table. First
I thought he was making eyes at her.
You know how Willie is.
She was pretty. With no warning
he started to laugh & cry.
Have you ever seen a man fight
with himself? For an hour he raised hell
with the waitress about ground glass
in his food. He didn't even know
who I was. Girl, it took three
cops with a white straitjacket
to carry him away.

A Break from the Bush

The South China Sea drives in
its herd of wild blue horses.
We go at the volleyball like a punchingbag:
Clem's already lost a tooth
& Johnny's got a kisser
closing his left eye.
Frozen airlifted steaks burn
on a wire grill, & miles away
we hear machineguns go crazy.
Pretending we're somewhere else,
we play harder.
Lee Otis, the point man,
high on Buddha grass,
buries himself up to his neck
in sand, saying, "Can you see me now?
This is the spot where they're gonna
build a Hilton. Invest in Paradise.
Bang, bozos! You're dead."
Frenchie's cassette player
unravels Hendrix's "Purple Haze."
Snake, 17, from Daytona,
sits at the water's edge,
the ash on his cigarette
points like a crooked gray
finger to the ground. J.T.,
who in three days will trip
a fragmentation mine.
runs after the ball
into the whitecaps,
laughing.

Susannah Lee

A Certain Reformatory

Today my bicycle spoke,
tomorrow I doubt
we will ever meet again.
On the blankness of this

plain, I've stepped up one
fortunate wish: to explode the circle
of denial, as it explodes itself
daily, by finer and finer detail.

This whole departure
looks bigger than my truest
fantasy: riding shirtless
through a certain reformatory,
my reformatory, where
all offenders are issued bicycles.

The limitations here are implied,
but by degrees
you will understand that
I was just a neighborhood kid
who dreamt of radio
talk-shows falling asleep, the

distant gossip of dreams opening
where the voice says go on, *go on*.
Then we moved. And when we moved, each

revolution made us heavy like husbands,
like rivers replete with
intuitive springs. Today I spent
a good deal of time expecting

to cross paths with you,
you my cursory jailor,
my sky with no brakes.

On Walk

The clockwork
can no longer

while daily the wind moves
down the avenue.

Handkerchiefs walk
like hands — there is absolutely

nothing I can hide from you.
Already the pigeons

blow up in fuliginous blooms,
I have named them all

Hilary. Watch, they will crowd
back on the solitary

timepiece. At arm's reach
angels sit concerto, and those

are easels tilted in perspectives,
the eyes of infinite

possibility. Walk with me.
In a movement of slighter

heartbeat —
a violin moans the park,

dog walk on strings.

Jan Heller Levi

Women

Of course we always want more than we have,
or less: the house in Maine, all windows,
and the water, like a pencil turned
on its side and pressed across the page.
In the dark night, we want to be a flashlight
or a cool breast for a hot baby.
Someone else's baby: Mozart at six, a little God;
or Tolstoy at eighty, refusing to see this century.
Of course we want to be remembered:
inspiring the poems, editing the poems,
licking the stamps. Where are our geniuses,
we cry. Our mothers taught us silence,
and, how we love them,
they taught us well.

This Is Not What You Think

"Beauty is to expose the cruelty in men"
— David Smith

Dangerous, the air we breathe,
the oily, roiling earth,
the skin we touch in desperate sex
and clinging. A woman in love is a pitiful thing,

so huddled into herself and hoping she'll fit.
Neither act
of will nor imagination can change this.
Locked,

unlocked, my darling, she craves
something inconceivable and gorgeous
as war:
guerilla clouds, wet waste

and shattered limbs. My God, you scream,
don't do this, but need is relentless.
You are a knife
I'm going to walk into again and again...

Philip Levine

Winter Words

When the young farm laborer
steals the roses for his wife
we know for certain he'll find
her beyond their aroma
or softness. We can almost
feel with how soft a step
he approaches the cottage
there on the edge of the forest
darkening even before supper,
not wanting to give away
the surprise, which shall be his
only, for now she sleeps beyond
surprise in the long full,
dreamless sleep he will soon
pray for. And so they become
a bouquet for a grave, a touch
of rose in a gray and white
landscape. All this 60 years ago
in the imagination of an English poet
who would die before the book
was published. Did the thorns
puncture the young man's fingers
as he pressed the short stems
through the knife blade? Did he
bleed on the snow like a man
in a film, on the tight buds,
on her face as he bent down
to take her breath? Did that
breath still smell of breakfast,

of raw milk and bread? What does
breath that doesn't come smell of,
if it smells at all? If I went
to the window now and gazed
down at the city stretching
in clear winter sunlight past
the ruined park the children
never visit, out over the rooftops
of Harlem past the great bridge
to Jersey and the country lost
to me before I found it,
could I cry and for what?

Blue

Dawn. I was just walking
back across the tracks
toward the loading docks
when I saw a kid climb
out of a box-car, his blue
jacket trailing like a skirt,
and make for the fence. He'd
hoisted a wet wooden flat
of fresh fish on his right
shoulder, and he tottered
back and forth like someone
with one leg shorter than
the other. I took my glasses
off and wiped them on the tails
of my dirty shirt, and all
I could see were the smudges
of the men wakening one
at a time and reaching for
both the sky and the earth.
My brother-in-law, Joseph,
the railroad cop, who talked
all day and all night of beer
and pussy, Joseph in his suit
shouting out my name, Pheeel!
Pheeel! waving a blue bandana
and pointing behind me to
where the kid cleared the fence
and the weak March sun
had topped the car barns,
to a pile, watery sky, whisps
of dirty smoke, and the day.

Kevin Magee

By the Inlet of the Infinitive *to Amaze*

for Margitt

The name of the boy is Michael, who rows,
his sister mans the sail. The storm, the boat,
the chorus' call for the boy to row it
ashore, hallelujah, slowly sung over.

We hear children master this gospel
and I wish all sight of the shore the storm
estranges that brother and sister from — home
or governed emotion — could by foresaken by them,

dedicated even to the threat of wrecking.
Last week I learned your name.
Already the run down cars that crowd the yard
next to the church we pause before forebode

the repose the threatened find if they reach land.
And yet, as perfect as the clicks a ratchet commits
are, the mechanic disrupts it,
swearing, flinging a wrench against the fender.

We looked away, and I saw white linen on the line.

     *

By the inlet of the infinitive *to amaze*
a royal palm's aroused crescents of shade
finger broken clothespins in a brake-drum,
and flies hum, owners of an overripe mango
caved open among sandspurs.

And chrome-flecks ignite and dilate
as midday's bladed light excises
them from hubcaps, grillwork, bumpers and trim,
and from the dirt's grey smear around a whitewall tire
the same sun sprays rare grains.

And love, ordinary as laundry for so long,
rips with abrupt excess
and limp cotton becomes canvas, a sail
careening hard against the heart's horizon
—bound to rebound upright, and abide.

The Inner Circle

He slapped her—just once, not hard—when she fainted,
and it's the shocked, ashamed way he tucked
his right hand inside that pouch between the calf and thigh
the body forms when it crouches

that makes me sure they have never
as much as thought of hitting or getting
hit for pleasure, in their secret life.
They're too young, although I heard the boy say

husband to the woman who asked him
exactly who are you? The same woman
who noticed the bandages on their arms and guessed
they both had been giving, selling, blood.

She said the girl had no business going,
she's so thin. Impossible to gauge
(unless, of course, you were him) how much
that hurts, how hard to say: We needed the money.

Sioux River

There was the bank and mud sloped into a sandbar
and what do you care?
Spare hooks in a shirtpocket,
nightcrawlers crammed in soil in a canning jar.

Supper, among your mother's family, was over.

Her sister went on and on about how poor
the past was. Their father's overalls, grime,
cuffs futile to try to wash; his work
on a well, which failed: pulley-rope-whir,
pipe-ringing, swearing, spit—a jangle

painful for the children to hear, way after dark.

And all you were good for was a slack tug
worthy of the bullhead that wound
out about 20 feet and then dragged
as always, on top: flaccid, slick.

Michael Milburn

Details (Wanting A Child)

A boy stumbles forward in the bus each morning
as his father, young and bearded, with a long body,
holds the door. Slowed by a snowsuit and questions
which must get asked, he allows people
to catch and help him, their smiles lasting
several stops down the road. In my lap, my neice

speaks to me painfully, half with words and half
drumming in what she must make known, and I surprise
    myself
scolding her like a wise, unhappy man
when she has said or done or eaten
something wrong. Her new sister accepts
the slugs and cuffs of her heroine ignorantly, answers to
    "baby",

and sags again on her useless shins, conveying
everything with private sounds and hands
which try to teach me how to yawn. And the boy I taught
    last year,
whose father thought good grades were genetic,
still hugged him seriously in the driveway at school.
They are something I cannot imagine

so I have begun to gather their details, as the snow
which has not stopped falling all week
collects about the door, turning my white car by night
into a hooded monster which feints toward me,
and by day into a ship a grown man might create
out of weather and threat of darkness, to ferry him forward

to an island where laughter is a mute gaping, and fear
a padded foot which hunts all the unaccomodating night
through rooms where the parent has gone.

In Weather

The Capitol dims and gives itself
to snow, and the trees turn their white necks away.
Couples loom, pause, and lose themselves
to words, long love, turning
to each other.

Lately, I've been losing you
in weather, not pretty thimble domes
but lack and need
We try to reconstruct the scene, the park,

then snow comes.

I wake with you awake
next door, the uneven rise
of voices in old films, and finger wide
the sharp Venetian blind as the dog-storm
moves across the triple-decker roofs.
Boston whitens silently and the voice
is a woman's, singing in the bath,
the long aimlessness of her song on tiles.

We take our scenery now
through thicknesses of wood, air or glass,
as you take me, a room away, the voices
real or not, ours or not, as far from us

as we are from weather, alone
at windows, and there is this feeling
of not being heard, of nothing being heard.

Laura Mullen

Letter

The words I try to write to you, pressing
The pen against your silence, against your silence
Fail. I should send you
The blank pages, with their blue lines
So near the surface (the places
You let me kiss you, inside the elbow,
The back of the knee...), or I should lie to you
As well as I can, saying, "it snows
A little each day," or, "there are no words in a white world
For this." I make up pretty good lies.
I walk for hours in the brilliant evening
Thinking how useful the moon is. I say *old bone* and I close
My eyes because I want to feel
How empty it is all around me. The night sky is so green,
And there are no stars, and where
The mountains break, black, on the curved edge
Of the sky the river turns back, the cobalt furrow
Of ice through the empty
Pastures still squared by barbed-wire fences
Stitches the snow to the snow.

Denial

We are not there now, we are never
Driving into the fog (in love but, having decided
This is wrong, not touching)
On our way to Stinson beach.
Taking the hard way, anyway,
There were road signs, CONSTRUCTION AHEAD
DETOUR, into a mist that became
Progressively heavier until, at last,
It was almost—caught in your hair, a hundred
Diamonds—raining. Like the rich
Woman you loved who stopped
Eating, I can deny this, it is
Something I have. So I say that the sun does not
Come out, lighting us in our awkwardness
(In our denial we've realized we do
Love each other), eating lunch on the life-guard's tower,
The other stray couple, and a seal, all
With the same flat light. I deny
That the past exists, thinking, I can't prove it,
Deny the body I held, holding it now
In my mind. We are not there now,
We are never standing together over
The head of a sea-bass we found—
Reflecting the sky, its eyes
Missing—washed up at the tide line,
Both of us looking carefully, thinking *this is something*
I'll use, later.

Debra Nystrom

Pheasant Weather

More than the rich white meat
or the feathers Grandma might use to make a hat,
there was some thrill in killing a gorgeous thing,
even in simply slamming to a halt
the car and all our desultory attention —
then the shot, and burnt trace of it,
smell that tastes of blood in your own throat —
The other drama besides argument.
I'd drop my comic and also come alive a minute,
despite the usual headache from Mother's cigarettes
and those hounding voices of the baseball broadcast.
As my brother trailed my dad's red shirt
out through the grain to fetch the dead bird,
I'd slump into my back corner again
while Mother rushed her private complaints and questions,
and I watched the immutable steely sky of that season,
not wondering why this was our one family event.
Not understanding this was my lesson in transport.

A Game

It was a way to toy with the warning
against playing in the woods at evening,
the winner being the one whose bike glided in
farthest, riderless, before crashing.
They all would coast down the three-block hill
with their legs tucked under and feet on the seats,
then leap where the road ends abruptly at the pines,
whose branches are so heavy, it seems
their own volition and not the wind that moves them.
Last night the first winner tore in after his bike
and found a dead girl next to it: breasts,
thighs and face smeared with red, wrists tied
to a trunk with flowered shreds of her dress.
He stared for a minute before flailing out,
and for those hours he might've spent with his family
or in front of the TV, he talked to the police.
His friends will no doubt think of another game,
but tonight after dinner the boy come up to his room
to watch from the window until there's nothing
beyond the streetlights' clear domain.
How suddenly and all together the cicadas begin.

Driving Home

The last birds rush, shadowless,
through evening's thick, sweet light
— color of honey, color
of the pine of our paneled ceiling,
beneath which I drowse too soon,
beneath which I wake at dawn
unable to recall my dreams,
and lie for my five minutes
staring at the pine's knots,
hurling the mind's useless hatchet
at the dark targets sanded flat.
To one side the window's black aspen
took shape in the glass again;
to the other you slept, hand open.
What is it that could have angered me?
I have home, I have love . . .
Still, the light by which I see
driving to work and driving back
is never daylight, never the clarity
that triggers the hawk's flight,
who views not simply grasses,
but the slightest movements beneath,
and seizes precisely what it needs —
while fox and coyote hunt
by watching that high, lone circling.

Bonin Drowned

Today I would like nothing
but the quick, violent breaking
of this storm that's crossed the plain
from the west all day, reminding me
of my schoolfriend Brenda's dad, Bonin.
The *Pierre Gazette* featured a photo
of the boat found below the dam, wrecked,
and Brenda must've known that week
how matter-of-factly the phrase
Bonin Drowned was read.
But maybe it wasn't foolishness
or the accident dealt
for being a drunk; maybe
he had simply spent another mute,
indifferent day of the kind
that go on there for months,
and despite warmth, comfort, lack
of irritation, he could think finally
of no one, no place,
no touch from wife or daughter,
nothing that would put aside the wish
to be taken by the water
and taken from himself by force.

Dzvinia Orlowsky

Praying

The priest taught us
that blessing oneself
shouldn't be like shooing flies.

There is a pause
at the temple of your head;

you connect one shoulder
to the other with a thread of light;

your wrist should be sincere
as if conducting your body
in song.

     *

On long car trips
it's okay

to pray while driving,
your lips parted

hands resting
on the steering wheel.

Soon, however,
you're falling asleep.

The rosary breaks
and spills into trees.

    *

Feeling guilty
for asking too many favors.

I disguise myself
by praying with my mother's accent.

Maybe for her
salvation will be gentle and familiar

as dawn pausing
to empty its grey sack of birds.

Anesthesia

The Cleveland Clinic advertises sun

so light you could kick
it with your tongue.

You board a plane: note the exit,
altitude changes, any difficulty
in breathing.

Morning slams
into the the taillights of night.

We will wait for you.

Yours are: a moon
hanging from a sleepless eye,

a small AM radio
pinned to your pillow.

Look:

they're beginning to descend,
one by one,

parachutists
carrying buckets of new blood.

One by one, the missing
are checking in.

Kevin Pilkington

Walking Home

(Amagansette, L.I.)

Each dawn this road beings
with a rooster clearing the pride
from his throat he couldn't swallow
all night. When trees notice me
they begin talking crow
since I know nothing of flight,
or how corn tugs you from cloud.
They are still annoyed
with a man who let them think Christ
back when he took the road's dirt
and changed it into tar.
I want them to believe in me
since I've also turned green
even if they swear bad food
or envy can never be spring.

After the last tree
sun is the friend I can use
greeting me with a breeze filled
with the trust I couldn't find in shade.
Here the road goes on
convincing me it ends at no door.
I keep walking as it runs
through a field that was once
an Indian burial ground.
Before tribes were chased, they left
their names to these roads

but each year their dead keep coming
back corn.

Sun begins tanning my shoulders
and when it grows weaker
I carry the rest of the day on my back,
past potato fields that add
starch to each breeze and a few pounds
to my lungs. Later a farm house
reminds me even here life
can go wrong, its wood the color
of drought and darker than the dreams
you can never share.

I walk over towards a river
to rest, then look in for the kind
of advice only water can give.
In a few minutes, I leave
considering the possibility of stone.
Back on the road a pickup truck honks a warning.
After passing me, I see a ghost
of dust follows it; the soil it carries
must be haunted with bone.
When finally out of sight, its horn
continues to echo in my throat.

Soon glass bends—their blades
aren't sharp enough to cut through
the threat rains sends. I decide
to go home before cows chew on the last
bit of sun and there is nothing
left to set over those elms.
I leave the road going through
an apple orchard that first looked
peach, then past a fence
where a horse wears a hat of flys

in case it does storm. And wherever
rain begins you can see it ends
in this field I cross, on a car
rusting in weed.

Untitled

I sit alone in the kitchen
thinking about my lover
who said it's over and listen
to the guy in 12B end
his binge with a song so full
of wine it sounds red. I pour
another cup of coffee, more mud
than the last, then look out
the window at the East River
and a gull who slides down
10 stories, bites off a bit of wave
then flys away dark,
polluted with tide. I'd blame
the river for her leaving
if I knew how to keep pain wet.

The room where we first loved
keeps coming back — her skin
still white and softer than swan.
We both found a place to start
things, soon understood that magic
comes from hands and not
from some star a sky shoots,
the way I always heard, over
an island too distant to name.
What pounded deep in my chest,
ribs couldn't hold; I learned
to follow it to her mouth then
let it loose in each kiss. Later
when we began falling asleep
still warm from the heat August
could never reach, my hands

filled with breast the way I wanted
prayer to fit. I could have
thanked church for her
and given it the credit I gave luck.

Someone in the hall coughs
me back to my table and the hack
in his throat keeps me there.
I begin realizing the kiss she gave
me last night can never
mean more than lips.
The singing has stopped, but next door
a tea kettle whistles again
at the attractive new tenant
walking past her stove.
In my living room
curtains the color of tongue
lick dust from a stick of light
noon leans against the wall
next to my uncle. He hangs
above the couch with the sorrow
of Dublin a photo has kept
in his eyes for 60 years.

Falling Asleep in a Town Near Beach

Tonight wind is so strong
I figure it's a ghost
that makes it howl and leaves
rustle until they scream oak.
It comes down from the graveyard
that overlooks a field
of condo now instead of corn.

Pox filled with fisherman
and farmer back
when the King kept the coast
colony and taxed your heart
if you loved. It scared
the village's first young preacher
more than lust then almost
made him wish luck
the night before he stopped
its spread with the right prayer.
He was able to push faith
again the first Sunday
after the last grave was packed.

The waters here were once deep
with whale and cod enough
to nail the village into a town
named after savages they chased
with guns, and when
their powder ran low — God.
That was before ships
began to tanker oil
then slick anything worth
catching away with spills.

When it becomes too late
for wind even to gust
I can hear the last train for New York
rattle nightmares out to sea
then whistle so many stars
out of mist they might cause dreams.

I begin listening to ocean
tell stories to the shore,
even though I know it's full
of surf, about tossing ships
and something about storm.
I then begin to fall asleep
soon after hearing the beach
snooze with sand.

More Than Blue and Cloud

The roof of my
ski chalet prays
for more snow.
Some fell last night
but lost
its virginity at dawn
to a skier from Maine.

In the distance
a mountain
shaped like a breast
on its chest of state
nurses a cloud.

And there is a hawk
or a dollar
the way it flies—
over woods
that are glass and elk.

A thin river
that begins
where no man walks,
runs fat with trout
gargling rock
clean in its mouth.

Winds rum my face
red and just north,
in the middle
of a story, 2 hunters
wait for something

to nail
on their wall.

I wish I could read
sky and tell you
more than blue
and cloud.

A red line
on my map
is the path back
to the spot I know
is chalet.
The tracks I leave
in the snow
might be trophy.

After the 3 inch hike,
I sit in front
of the fireplace—
its wood cracking
like gum
in the mouth
of a girl I once dated
from Clifton.

Her memory
brings a smile
and a warmth
this fire
will never know.

Trish Reeves

Goodbye

There was no air
and then there was nothing else
but air. This is called the filling
of the lungs for the first time.
The irreversible reverse
of this is when my mother calls me
and says: The flame fell off the candle
just like that.
And I say, Just like what?
And she says, I'm dead,
don't you hear me?

Of course I don't hear her.
I'm ten years old and riding
in my friend's convertible.
We're laughing at her mother
who is singing with the radio;
top down, no scarf, just singing
and every so often turning to the back seat
to give us a grin.

My old friend called and said,
My mother died. Didn't you hear me?
Of course I heard her.
I'm thirty-six years old.
I'm back in the fifth grade
on one of those Mondays
when the words were whispered:
Your friend's mother

did it again—jumped up on a table
at the Country Club Saturday night
and sang the blues. What do you think
your friend thinks about that?
I thought maybe she didn't know.
Not everyone's parents told them
about those party stoppers.
Although mine told me,
I was still so young
I thought the blues must be something
you sang when you were happy.

Rural Childhood

Do you want me to show you where the dog licked me
in the dream? But now that the dream's over
the act's invisible,
like water flashing its image
only when it moves in the stream bed.

My cousin took me to the loft of the barn.
We walked to the back
then he pointed down three stories
to the mud where the sheep fell dead
after a night next to damp limestone
in the dark basement of the barn.
I wasn't supposed to be in the loft,
it was too high. As I looked down
at the dead sheep, I knew I would never return
to even the first floor of the barn.

Sometimes crazy-colored cats lived in the barn.
But even news of litters of kittens
nestled in the hay couldn't lure me.
The news was always mixed:
not all the kittens survived their birth.

I remember standing behind the gate to the house,
safely watching, enjoying watching
the sheep shearer working at the entrance to the barn.
But then, with the first sheep running naked
from the shearer, they came back to me
in the form of multicolored air—those mottled kittens
that didn't live to open their eyes,
those still sheep in the mud,
the dog smashed in the road with its tongue hanging out.

And Then

It was an old river town
and then the river moved away.
Happens all the time: the river decides
it doesn't like living next to people,
there's a flood upstream
and the river takes its chance.

The problem with this is that some people
who lived on the river
are now seriously grieved.
They do not like waking up
to a line of sand
where the day before they saw bronze water
waiting to silver itself with the moon.

These people may tell themselves
it was not very good anyway, living
with the river. Not as though
the river was even the same river
from hour to hour. Now that they think
about it, the only constant was the bed.
That and the knowledge that the sound
earth and water make when they touch
is something to sleep by.
The sand forever in the making.

The Silver Coin

The cows once believed that if you stand in a pond
shaped like a circle
during the full moon
you'll die. That was everyone's first summer
and it finally got so hot
the animals decided to hire another cow
to go in the water. Just to be sure.
This was a cow nobody cared much about.
From the dry farm next door.
She squeezed through the wires one evening
saying there was no need for pay—
death would be enough.

She stood in the pond all night.

Now, during a full moon, the pond fills with animals
waiting for death. They call their pleasure
the other side of the silver coin.

Passion

I signed the letter, Mary
then noticed my mistake
and added: As you can see, I am going crazy,
I think I am a virgin.
Love, Mary.

There was nothing to feel guilty about,
it wasn't a bad letter.
I spoke some of my children,
a little of my husband.
While serious, it said nothing
about how serious I am.

No mention of the previous night
when seconds before I got into the car alone
I took a hammer and broke out
the windshield so life would be clear
as though through a clean windshield.

I wrote the letter as if worrying about God
mattered. I said, There's no sound
in my most immediate need: this air.
And there's also no desire.
But that's to consider
only one aspect. Don't forget the bitter
gesture of color—
no matter how many objects are struck by light
air is the same color when I see it:
silver not gold. My arms embrace air
the way my lungs embrace air.
I hold this stuff as if I need it.
But it could be water

I hold in my lungs
because as I know you've noticed
the air has no skin.
Holding it is like shouldering mirrors
in search of God.

Through the confusion I asked how her children were,
what had become of her husband
and how she systemized substance such as the breath
of those she loves.

It was a nice central letter
like one of those eggs
you put a small hole in each end of,
blow out the center and then decorate
for a religious holiday.

James Reidel

Kitsch

Rain falls on the carnival grounds,
the rides, motionless, loop the gray sky
with painted iron & height that would impress Paris
a hundred years ago.

They keep to themselves what death must seem like
when the soul leaves the body.

No one will make their money.

With the flat of his hand a drunken man
pushes the brake handle of his wife's leg
inside their trailer filled with the sound of rain.

Where is everybody? Far to the south,
in one of the casinos,
"The Hand of Faith,"
the world's largest gold nugget,
found in South Africa
& turned over by a man no better than a slave,
the pockmarked hand of a gold leper barely resembling a
    human hand
revolves in a glass case
slowly & stately as a pine scent tree strung from a rearview
    mirror

We turned away & saw the brass arms go up & down,
the engraved whorls of the carpet, the
gilt & lights that hide death,
& felt for our ridiculous quarters.

Week of January

A Christmas forest dies along West Ninth Street.
There is no disease.
Men come home from work,
drag the little northern pines
shedding their fishbone needles
down narrow,
carpeted
stairs.

Noble logs now, hirsute & dog-high,
stand at my side,
pettable—

Looking down on this thing,
I see my left shoe is scuffed & brown,
a potato shoe, an ornament,
its mate has a little fingernail of gloss,
the brown of joy.

Czechs

Popsicle stick is the diminutive of tongue depressor,
it is a serious implement to contemplate,
you reach with your little pink chocolated hands,
you want more —
my large clean hand withdraws what was once
the ice cream bar I shared with my baby son,
we cleaned it with our last licks,
& I dry it on my pants like a knife,
bundle it with the others,
the diminutive of *fasces.*

The rubberband is about to break,
it will break before we have enough
to undo bad history,
to complete the Eiffel Tower.

Of course, it will be made of wood.
Scaled-down.
It will be temporary, my son will burn it down,
& our lives are scaled down.
Short-lived, we are not immortal
France, the bare-breasted woman on the barricades,
we are Prague comparatively,
in comfortable circumstances unjustifiably
out of context, like other Americans,
not worthy symbols.

Norman Rockwell

When a child dies & it is newsworthy,
the newsman comes & searches the crowd, our eyes
for the delegate.
One of us
who can't wait to tell him before the heavily equipped one,
one like a soldier,
the cameraman,
"It is a shame, he had his whole life ahead of him" or
"He didn't get a chance to live" or
the women's variant, tears. Again,
Death, the ghost of the extinct wolf,
enters a neighborhood & someone's soup boils over
& someone's phone goes unanswered.
They stand at the edge of the lawn to watch,
their televisions flashing on the bare walls,
but the wash cycle ends without a witness,
the refrigerator goes on without a hitch,
the cat turns to its dish without being told,
& after we have made sure of ourselves,
after 11 o'clock,
the National Anthem at one a.m.

A Couple Playing in the Shower With a Gooseneck Shower Head; A Couple Waiting for Water Pressure So They May Cleanse Themselves

The plumbing hums in the walls,
white tiles hosed down for an hour now
in the room next to ours.

It is a copy of our bathroom,
it shares the same veins & arteries in the invisible kingdom
that exists inside of walls, behind mirrors & medicine cabinets.

She sits upright in bed,
her breasts hunker on bunched up sheets
swaddling her crossed legs like waves.

It is then the goddess appears to the sailor,
& she is as tall as a mast,
& his mast is broken,
& the only thing left of his ship
to hold on for his life.

He kicks in the water of strain that fills my eyes,
eyes that fill the inside of my head with swelling,
that head which fills her lap,
that heaviness of a basket full of stones.

Ray Ronci

Providence

At night
the hands come to the face
to push it together again.
The hands know the terrain,
have always known
how the years leave behind
fragments of the face.
The fingers push the layers
spread the skin around
rub the cheekbones,
find their place
closest to the skull.
Skin and bones of my spirit,
crawl space, temple, cave,
waiting room and cathedral
for many other spirits,
at night
the hands come to the face
and push it together
again.

For Mary

My sister phones and asks if I'm getting anywhere.
I say my house is full of ashes.
I tried to burn the whole mess away.
I realized I would die. I wept
and put the flames out.
It was a terrible mistake.

So I took a ride. Long by yards
by acres and acres of junk cars and things
not repaired but held. Towns
less than a quarter-mile long.
Dogs and more yards of junk.
So I came home.

I came home and moved away.
And now it's like being on the sea
because the trees cannot be seen,
because one sees only sky and hears
only waves in this room.

Outside, the light breaks up into clouds.
The smoke-like rain fills the eyes and windows,
glazes the empty arms of alleys and streets
held open and stiff. Mary,
it is 5 o'clock in the morning,
and I am definitely
somewhere.

Rilke's Waif

No place to lie down and say: home,
I live here, work here, grow and reap here.
No place to send myself.

So in this cold night
with a borrowed coat and a borrowed bike
I sit looking out the window of a borrowed home
and a borrowed wife.
And this body.
It gets later and later
and I wonder

could I come and lie beside you
and trade warmth
for warmth.
You sleep and snore lightly.
I'm afraid to disturb you.
What an old man I've become,

startled by the sound of my own shoes
hitting the floor, my own hands
coming to my face.
I sit far inside myself as if
an empty station where no one sweeps
comes or goes. I am bold no longer.

What initiation, what test, what trial,
for what reason do I circle the earth on foot
looking for a place to rest?
A voice says: Don't move!

I stare at nothing.
I cannot move. I cannot weep or laugh.
I no longer miss a lost family, my tears
no longer like a visit.

I have a little song I sing.
When I remember it
I'll sing it.

John Searle

Poem

for Hilary

In the lit room, an inkblot runs
on a napkin like antlers into
a three-quarter moon. Beginning
to speak, I...

gesture toward the ceiling, push
my hair back behind my ear, wait —
hearing a flower, red, blown
by wind as on a prairie, in summer.

Belt

It's been around a lot of times —
the orbiting of my life —
the notches
grow blacker.

Heart

It's got me.
Right in the heart
all this —

a nest —
made of broken things —
twigs and frayed string;

all my talk is a prayer,
my eye toward color looks out.

I Found Some Pennies
And Brought Them Home

for M.

A blue vein over fading bone, I kiss
your pulse. Whisper becomes breath
near tiny hairs. They're tipped, pinpointed
like stars in the kind of night that makes me turn,

like earth in a backyard garden
in early spring. Nights where
we ran. Our legs got tangled.
They seemed like white roots—feet dangling...

Alone, years later, I notice thin sheets
of ice over muddy puddles, the color
of old pennies. Pennies
someone dropped. They tap

like branches brushing against the only window
of an old shed, leaning far-back in the yard.
The boards are mossy, and a few rusty nails curve.
Including the pennies, we counted twenty-seven cents.

The early morning hours nestled, and we got
some sleep. On our shoulders, your hair
red as copper...my ear buried,
nearly breathing, higher up.

Robyn Selman

Used Books

The danger in buying used books
is the notes people leave in them —
like leaves, brittle, and coy.
This one, dated 1935, addressed: DARLING,
signed: YOURS; apologizes
for not being the French edition,
DARLING, on the way to France.

You are on your way to the coast.
I gave you an oversized Russian history,
which I should have made Robinson Jeffers,
but history is what you asked for —
raising the issue of getting or not
getting what we want from each other.

I have bought myself a guide book
to Paris while living in New York.
I am imagining how DARLING looked
as he said goodbye to YOURS.
She in her plumage of the railroad station,
he, with dust in his eyes
turning slowly to wave, slowly.

Still, you have gone to California.
I am on the way to France, yes,
in a manner of speaking only.
And this: two plates left on the table.
I can believe they would speak,
offer themselves another coffee, a match,
each to the other.

Conversation With My Father

When you died, I fell in love.
I have fallen into something dark
where every time I open my eyes
I am picking you up at the train station,
1965. It might please you to know
you are alive here, even if you never
saw this place. I keep
a nice home, learned from your wife.
I'm supporting myself and you wouldn't
disapprove of how. But for god-
sake, I knew you were dying and ushered
you out, too soon I fear,
because I couldn't stand watching,
and now this grieving
because I can't stop complicating the issue:
let go really.
You would like her,
she has a good heart.
You would flirt with her, I know.
I made two A's this semester.
I've been taking alot of pictures
of tiny plants breaking through stone.
Excuse me while I change the radio.
Yesterday I saw quite a sight,
it was a family shaped like ours
eating breakfast at a table.
The kids were both unhappy and the young
girl walked out before the meal was finished.
There were a lot of things I could have
told her, but said nothing, nothing.

The First Snow

fell early this morning,
long before we awoke
so that by the time we had dressed,
had coffee, there was no trace of it
anywhere.
All afternoon, I couldn't put my finger
on what was missing.
You said it was probably nothing
or only me distorting the facts again.
But in my usual way I read metaphor
in the landscape: the sky was hanging
so low. You got fed up with me
so I went stalking the grass and weeds
by the highway for one patch of evidence.
I kept wondering, what if I had slept
even later this morning—how
would I know that it snowed at all?

Whatever happens with us
I want to be sure it happened.

John Skoyles

Snowfall

This could be any city, the poor parts,
poverty both camouflaged and signaled
by unplowed snow. The morning paper
still lies on the doorstep,
touched only by the cold gloves
of a boy who moves in his own world
from house to house, past a silhouette
pulling a sweater on, to a woman
who answers her door in a slip.
Never have our neighbors been so stranded
in their pasts. One tries to get to work
and the sound of his footfalls
is surprisingly loud,
like pages turned in waiting rooms.
Another stands by a window
as the falling snow continues to erase
these streets where no one important lives,
leaving just the crooked shapes
of cars and houses, white silhouettes,
a background drifting forward, nothing else.

Against Autumn

Survivors return to the place
where something terrible happened,
crippled and set free
by the deaths around them.
They know they'll go too someday
so they won't go quietly,
and in this knowledge they stand out
like trees you never notice until autumn,
when the plain ones rage
and the common maple
seems to set our hats and coats on fire.
It's a season bothered by the untimely
deaths of strangers, a looking too carefully
for omens, coincidence, and signs.
A trail of party hats blows across
the expressway, and the traffic
seems suddenly exuberant, giddy.
Everyone marks death with bright fruit
from dry fields, fruit with a sweetness
too much like decay, or else impossible
to eat: speckled waxy gourds,
the spidery freaks of some rural imagination.
Autumn, when whole stadiums smolder,
and children, when you kiss them,
taste like the wind.
We have survived the pleadings
of the summer street
with its sirens, hysteria and beer.
Now leaves hang in twos and threes
like long-saved ornaments
at the corners of a tree.
Under that burly disheveling sky
mothers tell children life starts from a seed.

Front Street

Neither of us had an easy winter,
though it must have looked like it,
sitting at a window on the bay
with glasses of whiskey.
The low tide brought birdlife, dogs,
bits of clay or porcelain plate,
and tourists taking the lazy way to town.
High tide covered everything
right up to the porch, and one day
we lost our tempers over it.
Arguing with the powers of the moon
is a losing business and by spring
he went off to a high-paying job,
A.A. meetings, and no time
to even breathe the sea air.
I left to teach in a floral suburb
with the same detriments.
The tides don't miss us
nor the landlord who owned
that waterfront property,
nor Gerald the cat
who we squirted with pistols
when he crept up on the tern nests.
And Susan and Shelley, where are they?
The sea and its tides
must be having a laugh
on the two guys who fell
for their heroic example,
fatal to mortals,
of starting over and over again.

Karen South

Sleep Song

In these nights,
I lay on my side,

curl-up like an ear,
and wait

for the blank wafer called sleep,
the dark hesitation between day and day;

wait for the comma
in the white noise of life.

I have counted all my bones;
aloneness is cold.

I need you, father seed,
to come back,

to sing your sleep song,
that lullaby of endlessness

that sends me off without good-byes,
and sent the whiteness of my days

drifting out
like Chinese poem boats.

The Abattoir

In the drafty land of a day's work,
where bone saws sing
down to the tone of marrow,
these men in white coats
live out my dream
surgeons gone wild.

Outside, I hear the mallet man,
halting the morning between eyes
with his dull thud,
and the knife of the skinner
slips beneath hides,
the gliding hand of a knowing lover.

With steps muffled in sawdust,
I move through the rust odor of blood,
by the bins of heads and tails,
the pieces of a nursery puzzle.
In the pile of hooves
last steps cling,
negatives of prints
abandoned in some field.

Maura Stanton

March

Upstairs my husband types our wills,
Pressing the keys with one finger.
The sound makes eerie counterpoint,
To all the birds, newly arrived.

We have assigned our house and cats.
We've looked at our insurance forms.
The will must be typed perfectly.
The drafts are growing at his feet.

The typing stops, then starts again
While birds sing loudly in our tree,
And I remember how each March
The priest put on his purple stole.

March was Lent, the time of mourning.
I thought that it would never end.
I wished to be grown up, and gone
To sunny places, warmer lands.

Now March is short, but just as cold.
The birds fly off to make new nests
In trees they've never seen before.
I shudder at the tapping keys.

They strike the music of bequests,
Of bonds, executors, and graves —
Black notes across a legal page,
Meant to be played when we are dead.

Space

Monday a boy who cannot lift
Even a hand to wave goodbye
Comes to my office with his mother.

She has pushed him in his wheelchair
As she must have bathed and dressed him,
Clipped his beard; knocked on my door.

Now he tries to speak; he sputters.
Leaning down his mother listens,
Nodding at his urgent noises.

Then she tells me that he writes
Using his teeth to punch out letters
One by one, ten hours a page.

What is he writing? Yes, he hears me,
Twisting his face while his eyes shine.
"Another novel," his mother says,

"Space is his setting and his theme,
Stars beyond the firmament."
So she talks on. She makes me see

At once the creatures he prefers
Floating across the dreadful night,
Speechless in their metal casing,

Viewing the universe with wonder,
Silent brains, no flesh, no spine,
Amazing in their goodness, pureness.

All the while his lonely eyes
Behold us as we talk and gesture,
Mother, teacher, aliens, stones.

Terese Svoboda

Carwash kiss

The carnival doesn't rival the carwash.
For a quarter, I could get my brother

to ride on top and come out red as
a letterjacket while the spray steamed

through the window seams, a date's hand
cupped the edge of my Bermudas,

his lips opened on my neck. Then,
as it dripped dry, the doors still locked

so I could say things like where
next, my brother would start to holler.

Transformer

The train circled. You two hid
in the algae trees, slinking

around the plastic rocks, bellied down
to the liver-colored land, getting close,

getting closer until whose finger
grazed the tracks? Who cares:

you both reached the station sticky
with blue, the transformer smoking

and the train: crash! Daddy!
But that wasn't you.

You asked to meet him our first date;
I'd have married you for that alone.

When you gave me a ring, he got one too
and he carried the train.

You also had mother and father
only by halves: on the same shuttle:

summer, mother; winter, father.
Anger in secret; cry only on arrival.

Soon he had to have your mustache
pencilled-in for school and under it,

a tie your color. Those were the best days,
the last. First at the accident,

you checked his heart, his hand,
took his mouth into yours

for a kissful of air. From blue
to pink he went, pink, pink, pink.

Before the signal flickered again,
he was surely, for that moment, yours.

Lee Upton

Destruction of Daughters

The friend who is concerned
with backdrops, not us,
but what we stand against,
his way of looking at the women
he loves,
to not look at them at all
but at roofs, a bit of sky.
To understand when exactly
a woman is angry
because of the way she works
her mouth
he believes will never
be enough.
He opens the glass doors of his house
as the lawn steams with the music
of his daughter.
He has bought a piano
to lure her to him.
The music will never be obsolete,
a vision of the world
in a perfect rain.
As if two friends sat at a table
that suddenly appeared
with wine, the dishes
growing invisible
after they were finished.
A woman spoke—her voice so full of pain
they didn't have to feel pain anymore,
no one, not even that woman,

and such friends
could be direct. All that medicine
for your heart makes you lonely.
Friend, you might as well look
at your daughter, your one
instrument, as well as at the air
around her, dangling and streaming with music.
The music wants you both but knows
when to wait a little bit,
as if such a daughter cannot help
but be destroyed
and found again,
silent and then crying out, silent
and calling
and is that perfect,
that near a heart.

Hog Roast

If the town celebrates
his roasting
it's their right. He's their hog.
He's pork now.

His life in the mash has gone sour.
The bad fairy presides
over his crispy feet.
The prodigal has come back

and does not need
such company.
Now the fires licks this one all over.
Now the fire is giving its best

hog massage. Who will
eat this toasty face?
Corn-fed hog is sweet,
but sweet as a dog to the prodigal,

he's pork now.
And he cannot know better next time.
He cannot cry to the prodigal:
You, little one, shod

in your doubts,
run along to your gorgeous friends!
He cannot cry:
Let me see your back!

He's pork now.
So we can kiss — if we want —
his blarney lips.
So? So we're home,

barely edible,
lonely with the whole town.
So no one's lonely in hog heaven.
No one's got cooked feet.

The How and Why of Rocks and Minerals

And these others—what are they?
Not dolomite, sandstone, shist or calcite.
I might include ice—the colorless mineral,
if ice stayed ice.
But what is this one? Some go nameless,
do not look like their pictures.
This stingy lump, this once hot magma?
This is our whole cause
of trouble over arithmetic.
Now crack two of these together.
Fire won't start.
I've tried it.
How about this? The bad stone,
the go-to-work stone,
the stone in a uniform.
He wants to look just like the other stones.
But what would you call my new stone?
Nameless, anonymous,
this dark stone.
Do we think it will teach anyone
the name of the mountain
all these stones rolled down from?
To see the pool of water inside the gem?
Or is this the blarney stone,
what we get for our kisses,
for not knowing our rocks from our minerals.
This rock has a spot in it, so smooth
it is the start of the first quarry,
that zoo of rocks, the untamed, distant rocks,
the rocks that make us nervous.
On the Scale of Hardness we're talc.
But this is not fool's gold,

not banker's gold either,
our love stamped on it.
If this rock could talk I know it would
be quiet. Not a stupid rock,
this one we love.
The loudest stones of history,
they are sand now.

Ellen Bryant Voigt

Short Story

My grandfather killed a mule with a hammer,
or maybe with a plank, or a stick, maybe
it was a horse — the story varied
in the telling. If he was planting corn
when it happened, it was a mule, and he was plowing
the upper slope, west of the house, his overalls
stiff to the knees with red dirt, the lines
draped behind his neck.
He must have been glad to rest
when the mule first stopped mid-furrow;
looked back at where he'd come, then down
to the brush along the creek he meant to clear.
No doubt he noticed the hawk's great leisure
over the field, the crows lumped
in the biggest elm on the opposite hill.
After he'd wiped his hatbrim with his sleeve,
he called to the mule as he slapped the line
along its rump, clicked and whistled.

My grandfather was a slight, quiet man,
smaller than most women, smaller
than his wife. Had she been in the yard,
seen him heading toward the pump now,
she'd pump for him a dipper of cold water.
Walking back to the field, past the corncrib,
he took an ear of corn to start the mule,
but the mule was planted. He never cursed
or shouted, only whipped it, the mule
rippling its backside each time

the switch fell, and when that didn't work
whipped it low on its side, where it's tender,
then cross-hatched the welts he'd made already.
The mule went down on one knee,
and that was when he reached for the blown limb,
or walked to the pile of seasoning lumber; or else,
unhooked the plow and took his own time to the shed
to get the hammer.
                                By the time I was born,
he couldn't even lift a stick. He lived
another fifteen years in a chair,
but now he's dead, and so is his son,
who never meant to speak a word against him,
and whom I never asked what his father
was planting and in which field,
and whether it happened before he had married,
before his children came in quick succession,
before his wife died of the last one.
And only a few of us are left
who ever heard that story.

Visiting the Graves

All day we travel from bed to bed, our children
clutching home-made bouquets
of tulips and jonquils, hyacinth,
handfuls of yellow salad from the fields.
In Pittsylvania County, our dead face east,
my great-grandfather and his sons facing
what is now a stranger's farm.
One great-uncle chose a separate hill,
an absence in the only photograph.
Under the big oak, we fumble for his name
and the names of sisters scattered like coins.
But here is my father, near the stone
we watched him weep beside for twenty years.
And my mother beside him, the greenest slab of grass.
By horse, it was hours to Franklin County,
to Liberty Christian Church where her mother lies.
The children squabble in the car, roll on the velvet
slope of the churchyard, pout or laugh as we point out
the gap in the mountain where *her* mother's grave
is underwater, the lake lapping the house, the house
still standing like a tooth. We tell them how
we picked huckleberries from the yard,
tell them what a huckleberry is, but the oldest
can't keep straight who's still alive, the smallest
wants her flowers back—who can blame them,
this far from home, tired of trying
to climb a tree of bones. They fall asleep
halfway down the road, and we fall silent, too,
who were taught to remember and return,
my sister is driving, I'm in the back,
the sky before us a broken field of cloud.

The Farmer

In the still-blistering late afternoon,
like currying a horse the rake
circled the meadow, the cut grass ridging
behind it. This summer, if the weather held,
he'd risk a second harvest after years
of reinvesting, leaving fallow.
These fields were why he farmed—
he walked the fenceline like a man in love.
The animals were merely what he needed: cattle
and pigs; chickens for a while; a drayhorse,
saddle horses he was paid to pasture—
an endless stupid round
of animals, one of them always hungry, sick, lost,
calving or farrowing, or waiting slaughter.

When the field began dissolving in the dusk,
he carried feed down to the knoll,
its clump of pines, gate, trough, lick, shute
and two gray hives; leaned into the Jersey's side
as the galvanized bucket filled with milk;
released the cow and turned to the bees.
He'd taken honey before without protection.
This time, they could smell something
in his sweat—fatigue? impatience,
although he was a stubborn, patient man?
Suddenly, like flame, they were swarming over him.
He rolled in the dirt, manure and stiff hoof-prints,
started back up the path, rolled in the fresh hay—
refused to run, which would have pumped
the venom through him faster—passed the oaks
at the yard's edge, rolled in the yard, reached

the kitchen, and when he tore off his clothes
crushed bees dropped from him like scabs.

For a week he lay in the darkened bedroom.
The doctor stopped by twice a day —
the hundred stings "enough to kill an ox,
enough to kill a younger man." What saved him
were the years of smaller doses —
like minor disappointments,
instructive poison, something he could use.

Robert Winner

Home Early

I catch this glimpse of you
wheeling your shopping cart
along our empty street
I see your nakedness

And stepping from my car
with my briefcase, wanting
to catch you before you disappear
in the doorway, I also express
our odd jobs fighting the vacancy,
and the solitude.

Home

My heart and my bones wince.
It's so damn sad-looking and ugly,
The Bronx—
Driving past those small hills
Blighted for miles with brick
Desert-similar apartment buildings:
The landscape I come from.
It's so damn ugly in its torment
Of knifings and fires, I forget
I was happy there, sometimes,
In its damp and dingy streets, living my boy's life
With the five continents of the world
In my mind's eye.

Maybe it was beautiful before us:
A coast with no landfill, a bluffed
Peninsula of swamps and hemlock forests,
A wilderness that became another wilderness
Of beds and linoleum, school books,
Musty hallways, laughter, despondency—
Unremembering earth, a riverbed
Millions flowed on, clinging briefly
To some masonry, then gone...

*

I come from there, no landscape
To come from, no real hometown with leaves
And porches, drugstore and gas station,
No anchor in green, like Yorkshire
For Captain James Cook. I can imagine him
Returned home after circumnavigating

The globe, the South Pacific claimed,
Climbing the moors to find
His dreaming stone, his first South Seas
In that sea of wind-blunted grass,
Trees, stone farmhouses, barns
And near-emptiness.

But it's The Bronx I come from,
The Bronx that's washed away continually,
The landscape of hearts, The Bronx
Of spirit and flesh packed heavily
Passing through subways and doorways.
I come from there like the bus driver
Who tried to escape Gun Hill Road
Years ago in his red and yellow transit bus
And was found, days later, in Hollywood, Florida,
A girl in each arm, savoring the fruits
Of exploration in the sub-tropical sunshine,
Like Captain Cook.

Still Life

I think of my father
Working quietly at an easel,
With small strokes globing
The fruit and wine bottles.
How many breasts he painted
In pears and oranges and green glass,
Getting inside the blouses of things
Twice a week in the rented studio
He shared downtown.
The stillness of the subjects,
And their reticence, appealed to him.
They didn't risk too much
Emotion, like this poem,
Because, after all, we can cry for our dead
Too much: perhaps they remain as apples,
Fish on platters, bottles of red wine...

Thanksgiving Day, 1983

(On the decision to deploy
Pershing II Missiles in Europe)

All day rain beats like the war
On everyone's doorstep, war
That will have no location, no *theatres*;
Two weeks that nobody will remember
Settle the matter like a judge with one arm
Pounding out irreversible sentences.

Yet we eat and are at peace together.
The giant leech of tropical forests
Contents its hunger on nests of worms.
The armed horseman of the Elgin Marbles
Complete their ride; they end their long
Imprisonment in art and order,
Reach their enemies finally and slake
Their bloodthirst and are themselves
Slaughtered.

Franz Wright

The Street

On it lives one bird

who commences singing, for some reason best known to
itself, at precisely 4 a.m.

Each day I listen for it in the night.

I too have a song to say alone

but can't begin. On it, surrounded by blocks of
black warehouses,

is located this room. I say this room, but no one
knows

how many rooms I have. So many rooms how shall I
light

so many . . . Also yours, though you are never
there.

It's true I've been gone a long time.

But I have come back. I have.

Where are you?

I can change.

There

Let it start to rain,
the streets are empty now.
Over the roof hear the leaves
coldly conversing in whispers;
a page turns in the book
left open by the window.
The streets are empty, now
it can begin. I am not there.

Like you
I wasn't present
at the burial. This morning

I have walked out
for the first time
and wander here
among the blind
flock of names
standing still
in the rain —

(the one on your stone
will remain
listen in the telephone books
for a long time, I guess, light
from a disappeared star . . .)

— just to locate the place,
to come closer, without knowing where you are
or if you know I am there.

Oberlin

Audience

The street deserted. Nobody,
only you and one poor
dirt colored robin,
fastened to its branch
against the wind. It seems
you have arrived
late, the city unfamiliar,
the address lost.
And you made such a serious effort —
pondered the obstacles deeply,
tried to be your own critic.
Yet no one came to listen.
Maybe they came, and then left.
After you traveled so far,
just to be there.
It was a failure, that is what they will say.

Untitled

Rooms I (I will not say
worked in) once heard in. Words
my mouth heard,
then — be
with me. Rooms,
you open onto one
another in the mind: still house
this life, be in me
when I leave, don't take from me
what took so long.

Peter Yovu

Negative

My love is not an MX missile.
It is not a muskrat running in the suburbs.
A hen is not my love,
with its eyes of grub-intent,
with its legs of loose leather bending backwards.
My love is not a poacher,
shins hard as scimitars leaning on his ivory,
nor is my love the black bear's woof,
its muzzle of berries and mice.
A secretary coughs, expelling clouds of Listerine
and is not my love.
A downpour names a gravity my tongue should know—
not my love, nor love the ducks
and bottom-feeding fishes that swell on pollution
and the meat the poor could not digest.
A harbor is not my love,
licking its tugboats and pimps.
My love is not a Buick,
not a priest, not one finger pointing up from the rest.
A piano is played badly, as if someone had spilled
hot oil on the keys. Not my love.

Wind and Rain

This late at night, this late in the spring,
the north wall of darkness disintegrates,
shimmies into atoms swaying
on their chains like a curtain of glass beads,
each one amber to its insect of light.
Swaying, as someone preternaturally
thin and disfigured stands bestride them
waiting to be real;
                              yet beautiful if
only she would come through and be with me,
if she would stop smearing her eyes
upon her silks, stop swinging this house
like a lantern guttering on memories of hair,
like a lopped head through the city
my abductress invents as she goes.

First Death

She did not look maimed.
Heavy, slow, too dumb to stand and run
when she was knocked to the ground,
she took a gut-buster from the ram
she'd refused and groaned
and groaned if I lay a hand on her

and went on groaning as I stood,
strange in this life I'd begun,
and crowded by nothing but this decision,
I braced myself like a cop I'd seen,
arms straight out, fingers locked
around the blue .38,

stood half-blind with fear's
morphine crawling my face, like every good
guy's first dance with flesh,
whispering again and again
I have to do it, and suddenly felt
sleep's cold metal explode in my grip

as I knew all along it would.

Site

I went again to that place I loved
not far from here, or from the noise of cars
though quiet enough this early—
where the sound of a stream found
a deep ear in the woods, and came out
in me; went to that place
as one might go to the slain
body of a friend.
                    Mist,
body midway between pond and air,
stood long on those stumps, then rose
out of itself, in motions
a tree would know.
                    Then the sun,
indifferent to the taste of leaf
or limb, dropped its hunger everywhere,
licked the skin of water from the shadow plants,
the cowl of modesty from the pulpit jack,
the snail's canal...
                    Went again to that round
stone lodged in the thighs of an oak
where I used to prop my head, lover
to lover, one earth-bound, the other rooted
in change
                    and sinking my hands in the parched scalp
of the moss-grown stone, I tore what green
life remained away, exposed a cold skull to the sun
to warm whatever thought might stir within,
blessing or curse on the unbuilt house.

South Beach

We lived on the bottom floor,
four rooms in a new brick complex
(rooms stacked on rooms)
with a view of world enough:
the school, also brick; the paved
playground and remnant meadow
beaten to dust by Sears-shod kids.

Beyond was not our need.
From the gravelled ("No Admittance") roof,
we could see the small houses
of the Italians, fig trees unsheathed
for summer; we could see
the swamps of gulls and dumped
appliances, and far-off,
the glittering sea.
                    We looked down.
Our vision strayed as far as we could rain
mischief like pebbles on the girls.

I was twelve and I knew
Mrs. Regina hated her man, hated
his belly breaking out of his shirt,
his face raw in the morning.
When he'd come, drunk, huge,
home at midnight, pounding the locked metal door
with a crowbar, her voice broke through
the common wall: "I'll kill you tonight!"
"Scumbag!" he'd growl.

Sunday evenings he was pale.
Driving to South Beach he kept
a beer between his legs, two six-packs more
on the seat next to him; he kept looking back to see
if we, his son, his neighbor's son,
were happy.

We sliced heads off sandworms
on the concrete pier. Junk
wreathed the pilings. He drank beer,
stood staring, somewhere, somewhere,
and we pulled eels out of the sea.

Notes on Contributors

Ralph Angel's first book of poems, *Anxious Latitudes,* is due out from Wesleyan.... **Michael Augustin** is a young poet from Bremen, West Germany. He was in residence at the International Writer's Workshop at the University of Iowa in 1984.... **Tina Barr** lives in Philadelphia. Flume Press published her chapbook, *At Dusk On Naskeag Point.* She received a grant from the Pennsylvania Council on the Arts and has published poems in several magazines.... **Donald Bell** is a chef living in San Francisco. These are his first poems in a national magazine.... **Michael Burkard** recently received an NEA grant and the Alice Fay Di Castagnola Award from the Poetry Society of America for a work in progress. His most recent book is *Ruby for Grief* (Pittsburgh).... **Elena Karina Byrne** teaches high school in California. These are her first published poems.... **Richard Cecil's** first book, *Einstein's Brain,* will be out in early 1986 from the University of Utah Press.... **Gillian Conoley** has a chapbook out from Lynx House Press called *Woman Speaking Inside Film Noir.* She teaches at the University of New Orleans.... Two of **Della Cyrus'** essays have recently been reprinted in *125 Years of The Atlantic.* These are her first published poems.... **Stuart Dischell** has published poems in several magazines. He teaches at Boston University.... **Stephen Dobyns** is the author of five books of poems and five novels, the latest of which are *Red Dog, Black Dog* (Holt Rinehart) and *Dancer With One Leg* (Dutton). He teaches for the Warren Wilson College MFA Program.... **Edison Dupree** was a fellow at the Provincetown Fine Arts Work Center last year and has published poems in several magazines. He lives in North Carolina.... **Mary Fister** recently completed her MFA at the University of Massachusetts, Amherst, where she teaches writing and riding.... **Maria Flook** is the author of *Reckless Wedding* (Houghton Mifflin). She lives in Black Mountain, North Carolina.... **Alice Fulton** is the author of *Dance Script for Electric Balerina* (University of Pennsylvania Press). She teaches at the University of Michigan, Ann Arbor.... **Lucinda Grealy** won an Academy of American Poet's prize and has had a poem in *Intro.* This is her first group of poems in a national magazine.... **Jeffrey Gustavson** recently had a group of poems in *Agni Review.* He lives in Brooklyn, New York.... **Reine Hauser** works as an art dealer in Houston, Texas. She will be in residence at the Macdowell Colony this spring. These are her first poems published in a national magazine.... **Marie Howe** was a fellow at the Provincetown Fine Arts Work Center last year. She's published poetry in *Atlantic Monthly, Poetry,* and several other magazines. She teaches at Tufts.... **Richard Jackson** is the editor of *Poetry Miscellany.* His second book, *Worlds Apart,* is forthcoming from Grove Press. He teaches at the University of Tennessee, Chatanooga.... **Mary Karr** was the recipient of an NEA grant in 1983. She's published poems in several magazines and lives in Belmont, MA.... **Lindsay Knowlton's** poems have appeared in *The Boston Review, Intro, Tendril,* and others. She was the recipient of a Mass. Artists Foundation Fellowship in 1983.... **Yusef Komunyakaa** has published two books: *Lost In The Bonewheel Factory* (Lynx House) and *Copacetic* (Wesleyan). Wesleyan will also bring out *I Apologize For The Eyes In My Head* in 1986.... **Susannah Lee** received an M.F.A. from U.Mass/Amherst. She has recently been teaching at M.I.T. and Simmons College.... **Philip Levine's** *Selected Poems* was published last year by Atheneum.... **Jan Heller Levi** has published poems in *Benoit Poetry Journal, Pequod,* and *Extended Outlets: The Iowa Review Collection of Contemporary Women Writers.* She lives in New York City.... **Kevin Magee** is the editor of *Pavement....* **Michael Milburn** works in the Woodbury Poetry Room of the Lamont Library at Harvard.... **Laura Mullen** is a graduate of U.C. Berkeley and work of hers has appeared in *Ironwood, Sonora Review, The Threepenny Review, Poetry Northwest,* and others.... **Debra Nystrom** has published poems in several magazines, including *American Poetry Review.* She teaches at the University of Virginia.... **Dzvinia Orlowsky** has published poems in many small magazines. She lives and works in Cambridge.... **Kevin Pilkington** teaches at the New School for Social Research in NYC and has published poems in several magazines.... **Trish Reeves** is a graduate of the Warren Wilson College MFA Program. She teaches at Missouri Western State College and these are her first poems in a national magazine.... **James Reidel** is a PhD student at Rutgers. He has been published in a number of magazines and also edited a book of Weldon Kees.... **Ray Ronci** has published widely and has taught at the University of Colorado at Boulder. He currently teaches at Emerson College.... **John Searle** is from Moline, Illinois. These are his first published poems.... **Robyn Selman** lives in NYC where she works as an editor. These are her first poems in a national magazine.... **John Skoyles** is the author of *A Little Faith* (Carnegie Mellon) and is the director of the MFA program at Warren Wilson College.... **Karen South** does research in Hematology/Oncology in Providence, R.I.... **Teresa Svoboda** has had poems in *Paris Review, The Nation,* and many others. *Cleaned From The Crocodile's Teeth,* a book of translations from the Nuer, will be out this fall from Greenfield Review Press.... **Maura Stanton** teaches in the MFA program at Indiana University. Her second book of poems, *Cries of Swimmers,* was published last year by the University of Utah Press.... **James Tate's** most recent book is *Constant Defender* (Ecco). Two of his earlier books have been reprinted recently: *The Lost Pilot* (Ecco) and *Hints to Pilgrims* (University of Massachusetts).... **David True** lives in New York City and his paintings are represented by the Edward Thorp Gallery. His etchings are handled by Crown Point Press, NYC.... **Lee Upton's** first book, *The Invention of Kindness*, was published last year by the University of Alabama Press.... **Ellen Bryant Voigt** lives in Vermont. Her second book, *The Forces of Plenty*, was publised in 1983 by Norton.... **Robert Winner's** latest collection is *Flogging the Czar* (Sheep Meadow). He lives in New York City.... **Franz Wright** is the author of *The One Whose Eyes Are Open When You Close Your Eyes* (Pym Randall) and the translator of *The Unknown Rilke* (Field Translation Series). He teaches at Emerson College ... **Peter Yovu** lives with his wife and three children in Waterville, Vermont. These are his first poems in a national magazine.... **Thomas Lux** is the editor for this issue. His fourth book, *Promised Land,* will be published in early 1986 by Houghton Mifflin. He teaches at Sarah Lawrence College.

Barbara Einzig

George, The Name of a Fish

What she was resisting in him, or in his habits, or in his world of clothing and cars and books, she could not say. It was just important to not make what it was her own, and the only way to do that was resistance, an energy employed in constant tiny, invisible ways, with the aptitude of hemming, but with the confusion in the garment or body of their love.

Sentences became longer and more explanatory, their conversation more and more a proof in search of some theorem, their reason for or in being together. Finally she went along with some small part of what she had instinctively been against.

All of these things are trivial, domestic dioramas or shrines which only coinhabitants of a house may visit, or find. (Trivia was the goddess, he said, of the three roads, their meeting.)

One day the light of mid-afternoon, of mid-winter in a warm climate, filled the room as water does an aquarium. Here is the fish, suggesting what is necessary to take care of it.

It was his fish, he had bought it, having always wanted to have one, having always wanted to buy one. It was a Japanese fighting fish, and its exotic and vicious quality rendered innocent through isolation drew him to it.

She saw the green algae growing thick in the round, clear, moonlike container and purchased a snail, having read that they delight in consuming that very problem. The snail first sat on the bottom, on green gravel, but then began inching its way upward, and she saw the softness of its body through the glass, what was normally inside the shell.

Soon there was more than one snail, though tiny there were many, and the algae only partially cleared to reveal their small growing bodies among the green gravel, the color and softness of their young shells nearly identical to the adult body she had observed adhering to the glass.

If the world of the fish was his, he should be the one to clean it, and so she left this scene to develop, but occasionally she was so bold as to look at the fish, and the sight was disturbing. There he swam, but his activity lessened more and more each day, the fish dwelt closer to the bottom of the aquarium, site of the snail's origin, the warrior's kimono of primary colors fading with a declension identical to that of his swimming.

Finally she cleaned this out (this was her giving in), scooping and rescuing the fish in a cup designed for drinking coffee, and put him in a beautifully empty (except for water) bowl, being careful to first add a few drops of a liquid resembling water in appearance, but thicker, that makes tap water safe for fish.

The day the light looked that way what was in the jar she dumped into a colander normally used to wash spaghetti or lettuce, and the snails, unable to express their disgruntlement at the fall, were dumb there with the pea gravel. She threw all of them out but one, and then, after scrubbing the aquarium free of scum till it shone in the yellow sun brilliant in the kitchen, she returned the clean gravel, inserted a new plant purchased for the occasion, and added the fish, tipped slowly from its bowl, and more water.

She did other things too that let the resistance go, a rein, new things that were larger she went along with until suddenly

ERRATA

this amounts to submission.

All the energy previously employed in the invisible hemming, in the resistance to this submission, was then returned, an unearned gift miraculous as her own life, to her, she who walks out the door as she has so many times before but without this time returning.

Julie Agoos' poem, "In A New Climate," was inadvertantly left out of the Table of Contents for 10/4. The poem can be found on pages 190 and 191 of that issue.

Line 13 of Linda Pastan's poem, "Family Scene:Mid Twentieth Century," on page 108 of 10/4 should read:

"Pierre, I suppose, not Vronsky, with your passion"

In Gerald Duff's story, "Fire Ants," beginning on page 143 of 10/4, please strike out the repeated text from the top of page 152 ("Picking up speed....") to the top of page 153 ("She's in the house last I notice."). We apologize for any confusion this error may have caused.

Tom Sleigh

Hope

For Aunt Hope

Overhung by evergreen, your house was cool
Those afternoons the sun's long ghost shimmered
In the fading curtains. The rocker's senile
Back and forth wore ruts in the floor, the boards'

Soft creaking wheezing in, out. It's seven years
Since I saw you last for the last time,
Your eyes molten with remembrance's flicker
As events like magma poured and cooled, time

Confounding my grown-up face with your image
Of the photogenic, faded child.
Who was I to you? your bed barred like a cage,
A stainless-steel cradle, as in your head

My name roamed connectionless. And you too
Were strange, your hip smashed, your legs drawn up
And shrunken like a cricket's, your eyes' blue
Like clouded water in which I saw trapped,

Lost in terminal helplessness, the eyes
Of my aunt of childhood, ironic, clear,
And merciless, their killing-with-kindness
Stare that sent me to the boneyard hour after hour

Those endless afternoon wars at dominoes
Still lurking aloof from your stranger's face.
I held your hand and saw in the window
The two of us suspended beyond the glass

ERRATA

As through us waved a dusty branch, a rag
Of green wiping our smudge of color
From the air....Seven years, and your name still drags
Its luminous syllable like a lure

My heart still swallows, open-mouthed and hungry,
Its barb of light irresistible:
"Go fish in the boneyard," I hear you say,
Your eyes poker-faced, impenetrable.

Mercy Flights

Stories by Mary Peterson.
"These stories are frequently eloquent by way of what they omit: Peterson is nearly always one step ahead of the reader and often two or three. A very neat and skillful performance in storytelling."—David Wagoner   112 pages $7.95 p

Off in Zimbabwe

Stories by Rod Kessler. In a spectrum of modes ranging from the droll to the ironic, the stories in *Off in Zimbabwe* trace the problems encountered by a variety of characters coming to age as members of the baby boom generation, encountering many of the inevitable worms in the apple of life.
April   128 pages $8.95 p

To Leningrad in Winter

Stories by Steven Schwartz. Focusing on difficult transitions, the eight stories in *To Leningrad in Winter* present a variety of characters, each facing moments of loss and separation, fear and helplessness, will and desire. "Schwartz is clever, sure-handed, quick-witted, and deft as a stylist. He has the rare gift of being extremely readable, with that persuasive clarity of early Philip Roth."— David Wagoner
March   96 pages $7.95 p

Filthy the Man

Stories by Gerald Flaherty. "These are fine stories about men, mostly young Boston manhood, with not too much room ahead for high risk or honor, turning toughly round and round, picking away at courage. The characters—working-class (although often not working) sons and fathers (in general the wives and sisters go to daily jobs)—wryly mock themselves. Gerald Flaherty never mocks them. He gives us a piece of Boston in the way Joyce told us about all of Dublin."—Grace Paley
April   128 pages $8.95 p

University of Missouri Press
200 Lewis Hall · Columbia, MO 65211

TELESCOPE

A triannual compilation of fiction, poetry, essays, book reviews, and interviews devoted to the illumination of timely and significant topics.

**Edited by
Julia Wendell
and
Jack Stephens**

RECENT AND FORTHCOMING ISSUES:

Art in the Atomic Age. Jan. 1984
Focusing on the effects, influences, and anxieties of art and artists in the last forty years since Hiroshima. With work by ... Pablo Neruda ... Christopher Buckley ... Jeanie Thompson ... Albert Goldbarth ... W. S. Di Piero ... Marylyn Krysl ... William Pitt Root ... John Engman ... and others.

Literature, Cinema and the Image. Sept. 1984
Examining this question: What do the perceptions and techniques of film directors and film editors have in common with the styles and visions of modern and contemporary writers? With work by ... Rita Dove ... Maura Stanton ... Fred Chappell ... Denis Johnson ... Norman Dubie ... Robert Kelly ... and many others ... *plus* an interview with director John Waters.

Both *Art in the Atomic Age* and *Literature, Cinema and the Image* contain special surveys of contemporary writers' responses to the topics.

FUTURE ISSUES OF INTEREST:

Male Feminism; Avant Garde, Where are you?; Cult of Beauty ... plus open issues.

- -

TELESCOPE ORDER FORM
Published each January, May, and September.

☐ 1 yr. subscription, individual, $11.00
☐ 1 yr. subscription, institution, $14.00
   (Subscriptions will begin with *Literature, Cinema and the Image*, Vol. 3 #3)
☐ Back Issue: *Art in the Atomic Age* (Vol. 3 #1) $4.50
☐ Special Issue: *Literature, Cinema and the Image* (Fall '84) $5.50

Payment Method (Prepayment required):
☐ Check or money order (payable to The Johns Hopkins University Press)
☐ Charge My   ☐ Visa   ☐ MasterCard

Acct # _____

Signature _____

Name _____

Address _____

City _____ Zip _____

State _____

—Maryland residents add 5% sales tax.
—Foreign postage $3.25 for one-year subscription; $1.00 for single issues.

Mail to: *Telescope*
         The Johns Hopkins University Press
         Journals Publishing Division
         Baltimore, Maryland 21218

Writing in a Nuclear Age

Jim Schley, editor

"Anyone concerned for the fate of literature in the U.S. today, which means anyone aware of the impending death of our civilization, *must* read this book. *Writing in a Nuclear Age* is an anthology of our only collective hope."—Hayden Carruth

47 writers, including Denise Levertov, Grace Paley, Robert Penn Warren, Seamus Heaney, Maxine Kumin, William Matthews, Galway Kinnell, William Stafford, and Susan Griffin, explore the multitude of ways contemporary imaginative writing has come to terms with—or sought to evade—the acute sense of danger we all face. Dedicated to the potential for language to expose and comfort, prophesy and inspire, these writers have tried to restore to poetry and fiction their historic role as wellsprings of new thoughts and feelings.

"A resounding reaffirmation of the importance of contemporary writing as a moral force."—*Choice*

"There is little 'protest poetry' in this excellent collection, but much thoughtful consideration of what it means to be living in this unprecedented historic moment . . . This volume should be in every library, public and personal."—*Beloit Poetry Journal*

Reprint of a special issue of *New England Review and Bread Loaf Quarterly*. Paper, $8.95

University Press of New England
3 Lebanon Street
Hanover, New Hampshire 03755

This publication is available in microform from University Microfilms International.

☐ Please send information about these titles:

_____

Name _____

Company/Institution _____

_____

Address _____

City _____

State _____ Zip _____

Phone (___) _____

Call toll-free 800-521-3044. Or mail inquiry to:
University Microfilms International, 300 North
Zeeb Road, Ann Arbor, MI 48106.

Libraries & Collectors:

PLOUGHSHARES backfile sets Vols. I- X (40 numbers)

1971-1984 with index $240

Order from Box 529, Cambridge, MA 02139.

Announcing a Limited Reissue:

PLOUGHSHARES
VOL. 1, NO. 1 (1971)

Long out of print, *1/1* features David Ignatow Journals; *poetry by* Ted Berrigan, Anselm Hollo, George Anthony, Roberto Sanesi, Nicolas Born, Thomas Lux, Paul Hannigan, William Corbett, Sidney Goldfarb, William Doreski, Bruce Bennett, Bill Costley, Anne Waldman, David Gullette, Norman Klein; *fiction by* Carter Wilson, Catherine Dexter, DeWitt Henry, Cynthia Housh; *art by* David Omar White and Susan Smyly, *more . . .* "a major new effort . . . Highly recommended." — *Library Journal*, (1972).

Single copies $3.50, from
Ploughshares, Inc., Box 529, Cambridge, Mass. 02139